Portia tried  **detective as** **laces on her s** **Mick Campbel** **his presence a disturbing note to the already discordant evening.**

Exasperated, she met his gaze. "You're welcome to head back to the house if I'm taking too long, Detective."

"I've got plenty of time." A half smile eased some of the intensity from his face, and Portia found herself studying him. The dim light couldn't hide his rough-edged good looks. He'd be an interesting subject to capture in charcoal.

By the time she finally managed to remove her skates, her stomach was twisting with nerves. Murder. Just the word filled her with dread.

* * *

THE SECRETS OF STONELEY: Six sisters face murder, mayhem and mystery while unraveling the past.

FATAL IMAGE–Lenora Worth (LIS#38) January 2007
LITTLE GIRL LOST–Shirlee McCoy (LIS#40) February 2007
BELOVED ENEMY–Terri Reed (LIS#44) March 2007
THE SOUND OF SECRETS–Irene Brand (LIS#48) April 2007
DEADLY PAYOFF–Valerie Hansen (LIS#52) May 2007
WHERE TRUTH LIES–Lynn Bulock (LIS#56) June 2007

Books by Shirlee McCoy

Love Inspired Suspense

Die Before Nightfall #5
Even in the Darkness #14
When Silence Falls #18
Little Girl Lost #40

Steeple Hill Trade

Still Waters

SHIRLEE McCOY

has always loved making up stories. As a child, she daydreamed elaborate tales in which she was the heroine—gutsy, strong and invincible. Though she soon grew out of her superhero fantasies, her love for storytelling never diminished. She knew early that she wanted to write inspirational fiction, and began writing her first novel when she was a teenager. Still, it wasn't until her third son was born that she truly began pursuing her dream of being published. Three years later she sold her first book. Now a busy mother of four, Shirlee is a homeschool mom by day and an inspirational author by night. She and her husband and children live in Maryland and share their house with a dog and a guinea pig. You can visit her Web site at www.shirleemccoy.com.

SHIRLEE McCOY

Little Girl Lost

Steeple
Hill®

Published by Steeple Hill Books™

Special thanks and acknowledgment are given to Shirlee McCoy
for her contribution to THE SECRETS OF STONELEY miniseries.

To Seth, whose honesty inspires me and whose gifts
never cease to amaze me.

To Beth Sharo. If we weren't sisters, we undoubtedly
would have been friends. What a blessing to be both!

And to Rodney. Just because.

STEEPLE HILL BOOKS

Steeple
Hill®

ISBN-13: 978-0-373-44230-0
ISBN-10:   0-373-44230-0

LITTLE GIRL LOST

Be at rest once more, O my soul, for the Lord has been good to you. For You, O Lord, have delivered my soul from death, my eyes from tears, my feet from stumbling, that I may walk before the Lord in the land of the living.

—*Psalms* 116:7–9

But thy eternal summer shall not fade,
Nor lose possession of that fair thou ow'st,
Nor shall death brag thou wander'st in his shade,
When in eternal lines to time thou grow'st,
So long as men can breathe, or eyes can see,
So long lives this, and this gives life to thee.
        —*William Shakespeare,* "Sonnet 18," lines 9–14

ONE

She was going to have fun if it killed her. And, judging by the way Portia Blanchard's feet were slipping out from under her, it just might.

"Come on, Portia. You can do better than that." Her older sister Cordelia laughed the words as she sped by Portia, her skates spraying chips of ice as she passed.

"Your skirt is too long and too full. That's why you're having trouble. Let's go back to the house. You can change clothes." Miranda, the oldest of Portia's five sisters, took her arm, urging her toward the edge of the pond.

"Changing won't transform me into a world-class skater, Miranda." Portia pulled away, her clumsy efforts almost landing her on the ice. She'd never been graceful on skates, but she'd always loved trying. Loved the yearly twilight skate she shared with her five sisters, loved the cold crisp air, the feeling that no matter what the future held, they had each other. "Besides, I don't want to miss sunset."

"We've still got twenty minutes until sunset. That's plenty of time to get to the house and back." Miranda was nothing if not determined.

"Twelve minutes. Give or take a few seconds,"

Bianca, second-born and usually the peacemaker of the family, cut in. "She's an adult, Miranda, not a kid. She can wear what she wants, so stop nagging her."

"I was *not* nagging. I was just pointing out that pants might be more appropriate."

"Appropriate? Since when has Portia been appropriate?" Nerissa skated toward them, a smile lighting a face so like Portia's even their father had difficulty telling them apart.

"Since never." Juliet joined them. The baby of the family, she had a restless energy that was never quite contained, though tonight she seemed subdued, her green eyes lacking their normal sparkle.

They all seemed subdued and Portia knew she was partially to blame, her heartache adding to the discordant note of this year's reunion. Maybe she should have stayed in New York. The family had enough to worry about without adding her troubles to the mix.

"No, you shouldn't have stayed in New York." Rissa leaned in close, sensing her thoughts and whispering the reassurance in her ear.

"No twin secrets tonight." Juliet smiled, but there was something in her eyes that bothered Portia. Sadness? Jealousy? "We're here to have fun and relax. So why are we all looking so gloomy?"

The question hung in the air, no one willing to give voice to the answer. After almost twenty-three years of believing their mother dead, they had evidence that she might be alive. It was *she* who occupied their minds this cold February day. But more than that occupied Portia's.

She thought of Tad, of Jasmine, of the wonderful time they'd had together at last year's Winter Fest, and felt something hot and tight fill her chest. *"You're* all looking gloomy because none of you can compete with my grace and beauty on the ice."

She whirled away from her sisters, attempting a spin that athletic Delia could have done in her sleep, but that Portia had never perfected. Her skirt billowed out, tiny silver mirrors sewn into the material catching the last rays of golden sunlight. For a moment she was fluid and graceful, the world reduced to a smeared painting she longed to capture on canvas—powdery snow, towering evergreens, a hazy purple sky. Then her feet tangled and she flew backwards, landing in a heap of fabric, laughter bubbling up and spilling out. If it was edged with hysteria, only Rissa would hear and she'd never dream of pointing it out.

Detective Mick Campbell followed the sound of laughter across a road and through a cove of trees. Unless he missed his guess, the pond he was looking for was just ahead. According to Winnie Blanchard, all six of the Blanchard sisters were skating there. A thin layer of snow muffled his footsteps as he moved into a clearing shadowed in twilight. The pond, much larger than Mick had expected, shimmered in the fading light. As Winnie had said, six women were in the center of the ice. Five stood with their backs to Mick. The sixth sat in a puddle of bright fabric, laughing up at her sisters. Mick had the impression of wide, dark eyes, finely drawn features and curly hair pulled back from a pale face.

Which sister was she? Not Miranda. Mick had known the eldest of the six in high school and had seen her once since his return to Stoneley nine months before. Bright colors weren't her style. Neither was loud laughter. If memory served, Juliet had fair hair and light eyes. He'd seen pictures of Bianca in recent weeks. This wasn't her. That left Cordelia and the twins—Nerissa and Portia.

The woman sitting on the ice laughed again, extending her hand to one of the other women and allowing herself to be pulled upright. Perhaps she sensed his gaze. One minute she was laughing, the next she fell silent. Even from a distance Mick could see her body stiffen, her back straighten. She turned her head, glancing up the slope of the hill where he stood.

He raised a hand in greeting and strode forward, not quite catching what she said to her sisters. Whatever it was had them turning as one to watch his approach.

"Hello, can we help you?" She called out to him, gliding forward a few inches before slipping and landing in a heap on the ice once again. This time she didn't laugh, though Mick was sure she wanted to.

"I'm Detective Mick Campbell. Stoneley Police Department."

"What can we do for you, Detective?" She struggled to her feet as her sisters started toward the edge of the pond.

"I'm investigating the death of Garrett McGraw. I've got a few questions I'd like to ask your family."

"According to the newspaper, Mr. McGraw was drunk and drove off a cliff. I don't see what that has to do with us." Bianca Blanchard stepped off the ice and sat on a wood bench, her dark eyes calm.

"Garrett McGraw was dead before his car went over the cliff."

"Heart attack?" Bianca pulled on boots and stood.

"He was murdered." Mick watched for a reaction, scanning the faces of each of the sisters, hoping to glimpse guilt or innocence in their expressions. His gaze was caught and held by the only sister still on the ice. She moved gingerly, wobbling on skates she obviously wasn't use to, her forehead creased with concentration. Unlike her sisters, she lacked a natural grace on ice, though her gentle beauty and guarded expression made Mick want to look closer.

"Murdered? Are you sure?" Bianca spoke, pulling Mick's attention back to the conversation.

"Unfortunately." Things would have been easier if the answer had been a different one. A man like McGraw made as many enemies as he did friends. Finding the person responsible for his death might prove difficult, though Mick was determined to do so. He owed his ex-partner that much.

"And you think this has something to do with our family?" It was Miranda who spoke this time, her concern obvious.

"Your father and aunt are waiting at the house. Why don't we discuss it there?"

"Why don't you tell us what you suspect? Then maybe we'll talk." Another one of the sisters spoke, her short hair spiking out from under the knit cap she wore.

"Because the house is a much warmer place to talk, Delia." Miranda pushed her feet into black snow boots. "I, for one, could use a cup of coffee."

"Coffee would be good. Are you okay, Portia?" Bianca grabbed her skates and turned toward the pond. Mick followed the direction of her gaze, saw the skirt-wearing sister still easing toward the edge of the ice.

"I'm fine. Just give me another minute."

Portia. He should have known. The name fit the woman, its exotic sound matching her interesting choice of clothes. Despite three years spent avoiding women and relationships, Mick was intrigued. As he watched, she stepped off the pond, her feet wobbling, her gaze on her sisters rather than the ground. He knew what would happen next and moved toward her.

A few questions he wanted to ask the family? The detective made it sound so innocuous, his relaxed manner belying the seriousness of what was happening. Obviously, if he didn't suspect her family was involved in Garrett McGraw's murder, Detective Campbell wouldn't be here. Portia tried to convey her fear silently to her sisters, but they all seemed intent on grabbing skates and moving toward the path that led back to Blanchard Manor. She'd have to say something. That was all there was to it. "I—"

Before she could finish, her ankle twisted under her and she tripped, bracing herself for the third fall of the evening. Instead, hard fingers gripped her arm, pulling her upright. "Whoa! Careful."

"Thanks." Portia looked up into clear blue eyes and a face as cold and implacable as Maine in the winter. She didn't know what she'd been hoping for—compassion? Softness? Some sign that he wasn't here to destroy her family? It wasn't there. All she saw was determination and what looked like anger burning beneath his cool gaze.

"No problem." He stepped back, putting distance between them, though he watched her intently, as if waiting for her to stumble again. She hoped she'd disappoint him, but the skates twisted as she took an unsteady step toward the bench.

He grabbed her arm again. "Keep it up and you'll break your ankle."

"It wouldn't be the first time."

He stared into her eyes for a moment, then smiled, the slow upward curve of his lips causing her heart to stall and start up again.

"Why doesn't that surprise me?"

"Because you've seen how graceful I am?"

"Let me help you, Portia." Rissa grabbed her hand, squeezing twice, the silent communication they'd perfected as children and still used on occasion. *What are you doing?*

What *was* she doing? Her family might be in serious trouble, the business her grandfather had worked so hard for in for more of the bad publicity it had garnered a few weeks ago when Howard Blanchard had crashed his sister's sixtieth birthday party. The girls' grandfather and family patriarch, he'd once been the pillar of the community. Despite that, or perhaps because of it, his wild accusations and incoherent ramblings had made him tabloid news. The gossip was finally dying down. Portia wanted to keep it that way. Which was why she should not be joking with a man determined to dig up more trouble for her family.

She shot a look at her twin, shrugged her shoulder in response to her questioning look and hurried over to the bench, trying her best to ignore the detective as she fought with the laces on her skates. Unfortunately, he was hard to ignore, his intense stare making her fingers fumble on the laces.

Exasperated, she met his gaze. "You're welcome to head back to the house if I'm taking too long, Detective."

"I've got plenty of time." A half smile eased some of the intensity from his face, and Portia found herself studying the craggy planes and deep hollows of his

cheeks, the dark stubble on his chin and the fine lines
that fanned out from his eyes. The dim light couldn't
hide his rough-edged good looks. He'd be an interesting subject to paint. Or better yet, to capture in charcoal.

He raised an eyebrow and she dropped her gaze, heat
creeping up her neck and into her cheeks. She could sense
his impatience, the impatience of her sisters who hovered
at edge of the woods. By the time she finally managed to
remove her skates and pull on her mukluks, her heart was
pounding with anxiety, her stomach twisting with nerves.
Murder. Just the word filled her with dread.

"Are we ready?" Rissa grabbed the skates from the
place where Portia had dropped them. "I'm freezing."

"Me, too." Portia stood, started to follow her retreating sister and was pulled up short by a tug on her skirt.
A jagged piece of wood had caught the silky material
and she leaned down to free it as icy wind blasted across
the clearing, knifing through the clothes she'd layered
herself in. She shivered, tugged at the cloth.

"Let me help." The masculine voice sounded so close
to her ear that Portia jumped, turning to face the detective who stood just inches away. His eyes were even
bluer than she'd thought, his hair a short, spiky golden-
brown that looked as if it would be soft to the touch.

That she would even think such a thing had Portia
stepping back, dropping her eyes away from his knowing gaze. "I thought you'd gone on ahead."

"And leave you out here by yourself?"

"It wouldn't be the first time I'd been out here alone."

"But it may be the first time you've been out here
alone while a murderer wanders free." He leaned forward and peered at her skirt. "Why don't you let me do
that for you?"

"Thanks, Detective, but I think I can handle it. And I really am okay out here alone." At least she always had been before. As a child, she'd often wandered the grounds of Blanchard Manor long after the sun had set, but the deepening twilight and dark woods suddenly seemed sinister and foreign.

"Everyone around here calls me Mick." As he spoke, he brushed her hands away from the material and worked it free.

"Mick, then. Thanks for the help. Again."

"No problem. Again. Come on. Let's catch up to your sisters." He offered his hand, his eyes hard to read in the fading light.

She hesitated and then linked her wool-covered fingers with his leather-covered ones. It was a bad idea. Holding hands with a man was high on her list of things she shouldn't ever do again. Hadn't that been how her relationship with Tad had started—a brush of his fingers against hers as they'd chatted about Jasmine's progress in the art class Portia was teaching? The next thing she knew, they were strolling through her arts-and-crafts store laughing about something she couldn't even recall.

"Relax. I don't bite." His voice broke into her thoughts, the hint of laughter in it a surprise.

"Maybe not, but you *are* investigating my family and that makes me uncomfortable."

"Why? Do you have something to hide?" The laughter was still there, though Portia sensed an intensity to the words, a stillness to the man that let her know he was weighing her comments and responses.

"No."

"Then you've got nothing to worry about. Besides, I'm investigating a murder, not your family."

"Yet, you're *here*. You must think there's some connection."

"Not yet. That's what I'm trying to determine." He ushered her onto the path that led through the trees.

"I can tell you the answer to that right now. Investigating my family is a waste of time. No one in it would commit murder."

"And I can tell you that half the people I interview say the same thing. A good majority of them are wrong."

What could she say to that? That she trusted her sisters, her aunt? Her father? That she'd never been betrayed, or lied to, or discovered that someone she believed in didn't deserve her confidence? She had. It was a lesson she'd learned hard and well and had no intention of repeating, but that wasn't something Mick needed to know.

The sound of branches breaking up ahead saved Portia from saying anything at all. Mick's hand tightened on hers and he pulled her off the path and into the deep shadows of the trees.

"What—?"

"Shhh. Let's see who it is before we make our presence known." He whispered the words, his lips close to her ear, his breath warm against her cheek. She could feel the tension in his muscles, the coiled strength. Another branch snapped and Portia jerked, bumping against Mick, her heart thrumming a rapid beat. His arm came around her, pulling her close against his chest. She allowed it, her mind filled with visions of masked murderers stalking through the trees.

"Portia?" Rissa's voice carried through the trees, and Portia sagged with relief.

"Right here." She pulled her hand from Mick's and

stepped back onto the path. Twilight filtered through the trees coloring them in purplish light. The effect was eerie, the hazy glow shifting around the shadowy figure that stood a few yards away. Rissa? It had to be, yet a trick of light warped her figure, making her seem taller, bulkier. More sinister.

"There you are." Her twin stepped closer, her stylish wool coat and bright knit hat now visible. "Everyone else is already at the house warming up. What's taking so long?"

"I got tangled up with the bench." Portia strode forward, breathless, still nervous for reasons she couldn't name. "Mick was kind enough to help me out."

"It wasn't a problem."

"That's good to know. Portia tends to get tangled up with things, so having an extra set of hands around to free her is great news for me." Rissa's words were light and teasing, but Portia could sense the anxiety that radiated from her twin. As laid-back and low-key as Mick seemed, he was there for a reason. They both knew it, and Portia was sure, were both worried about what he might find. Until recently, they'd believed their family story to be mundane. The tragedy of their mother's death was so far removed from their lives they felt it in only the most indirect ways. Now, what had seemed mundane had become a mystery and everything they'd believed to be true was a lie.

How that related to Mick's murder investigation, Portia didn't know, but she had a sick, horrible feeling a connection was there. And when Mick found it, there might be very little she could do to save her family.

TWO

Blanchard Manor stood like a stone sentinel guarding the cliffs that jutted above the Maine coastline. Over a hundred years old, the house had become an icon in Stoneley, symbolizing the strength and fortitude of the people who'd carved lives from the harsh ocean and craggy earth. To Portia, it symbolized something else entirely—a way of life she refused to be part of, a cold formality that stifled warmth and emotion. As a child, she'd dreamed of leaving the Manor, of making a name for herself in the community of artisans that lived in Stoneley. It hadn't taken her long to realize that her father's influence extended into the town and beyond and that if she ever wanted to become her own person, an artist in her own right, she'd have to go much farther than the town she'd loved.

New York had seemed the perfect place to find herself. And she had for a while, enjoying the novelty of opening her arts-and-crafts store, of teaching art to young students, of being Portia the artist rather than Portia, Ronald's daughter. Still, each time she returned to the Manor, she was reminded of old dreams and even older wounds, of an emptiness that she'd never quite been able to fill, a longing to be accepted for who and what she *was* instead of being judged for what she *wasn't*—the perfect daughter willing to take her place in the family business.

"We're in the drawing room." Aunt Winnie called out from the room to the right of the front door as Portia stepped into the house, and Portia felt a twinge of guilt. Winnie had been so good to her, so good to *all* of them. Who was she to complain about what she hadn't had when what she had received from her aunt had been so rich in affection?

"We're coming." She pasted on a smile and followed Rissa across the foyer, hoping no one inside the drawing room would sense her melancholy mood.

"You okay?" Mick pulled her to a stop outside the door, his words just for her.

"I'm great." She met his gaze, keeping the smile in place even as his light blue eyes speared into hers. Could he see what she was hiding? The part of herself that wanted to be anywhere but where she was right now? "We'd better go in before Father comes looking."

"'Father?'" He cocked his head, letting his gaze travel from her fluffy pink earmuffs to the mukluks that covered her feet.

"What?"

"You don't look like the 'father' type."

"What type do I look like?"

"Dad, Pops, something a lot less formal."

He was right. *If* she'd lived in a different house, with a different father. She turned away, not wanting him to see the truth in her eyes. "We're a formal family."

"Yeah, I sense that." Mick let his gaze wander the oversized foyer they were standing in. Marble tiles glistened beneath his feet, a crystal chandelier hung overhead and a large round table took center stage. A vase of red roses added color, but did little to soften the museum-like feel of the place. It was a far cry from the comfortable, lived-in Queen Anne he'd grown up in, or the well-worn Cape Cod he now owned. A far cry from what he imagined Portia's home looked like.

He stepped into the drawing room behind her, watched as she sat on a wide velvet ottoman in a corner of the room. She could have taken a seat on the couch next to her twin and Delia, a rocking chair between the chairs Bianca and Juliet were seated in, the loveseat where her father and his newest girlfriend sat or the wing-backed chair that matched the ones Miranda and Winnie were in. Instead, she'd taken a place just on the edge of the circle created by her family, her shoulders tense as if ready to do battle. Interesting.

"Good. We're all finally here. Let's get this over with. Alannah and I have plans for this evening." Ronald's voice whipped out, filled with impatience, and Mick turned to the older man.

"This won't take long, Mr. Blanchard."

Ronald shrugged, his black eyes giving away nothing of what he felt. "Why don't you have a seat and tell us why you're here. You said something about a private investigator?"

"As I told you earlier, Garrett McGraw was killed two weeks ago. I'm investigating his death."

"And?"

"He was murdered." Mick kept his voice even and his tone neutral. He wasn't here to make accusations. Yet.

"So my daughters told me, but I don't see what that

has to do with my family." He was lying. Mick could see it in the subtle shifting of his eyes, the quick glance he shot Bianca's way.

"I have reason to believe Mr. McGraw had business dealings with one of your daughters."

"Any dealings he had with my family are private, Detective."

"They might have been before Garrett's murder. Now things have changed."

"I'm afraid we're going to have to agree to disagree." Ronald stood, his obsidian eyes flashing a challenge. "Now, if you don't mind—"

"We've got nothing to hide, Father." Bianca cut in, shooting Ronald a look that might have been a warning. "No reason not to tell the detective what we know."

When she turned her attention to Mick, she was all business, her expression cool and unperturbed. "I hired Garrett McGraw to find information about our mother. I'm sure you've seen the story in the local papers."

"I have."

She nodded. "Then you know he found evidence that our mother might be alive."

"And that some people are claiming her death was an elaborate cover-up, that the family might not have wanted to admit she had mental-health issues. Yes, I know."

"Cover-up! What kind of newspapers are you reading?" Ronald's face reddened, his hands fisting at his sides.

"Specifically? The one that paid him several thousand dollars for his story."

"And you believe that garbage?" Ronald shook his head, apparently disgusted, though Mick was sure he saw fear in the man's eyes.

"What I believe is that Garrett McGraw was working for your family. He found information that you might have preferred to keep hidden. Now he's dead. According to his weekly planner, he was to meet with someone in your family two days before his death. I'm wondering if that meeting took place."

"It did. I paid him for the information he'd found." Bianca spoke quickly, as if afraid her father might say something that disagreed with her account.

"And he didn't ask for more?"

"More money? No. I asked him to continue investigating. He agreed." Bianca looked puzzled, and Mick was sure she knew nothing of McGraw's reputation. Most people didn't. Which was the way McGraw had wanted it and the way Mick felt obligated to keep it.

"So you had no idea he was planning to sell your family's story to the tabloids?"

"Of course not."

"If you're implying that my sister knew what Mr. McGraw planned to do and committed murder to keep him quiet, you're way off." Portia spoke up, her voice quiet but firm, her dark eyes staring into his as if she could read whatever motive he might have.

"I'm not implying anything. I'm asking."

"And I'm telling you that Bianca would never commit a crime. I doubt she's ever even gotten a parking ticket."

"I'm not that perfect, Portia." Bianca smiled at her younger sister, and Mick saw the affection between them. Obviously, it wasn't Portia's relationship with her sisters that had her sitting at a distance. So maybe it was her father that she had a problem with. Or his girlfriend.

"I didn't say you were perfect. I said you weren't a murderer." Portia rose and paced across the room, tiny bells jingling at her wrist as she swept a hand over her hair.

"My questions are standard. I'm not accusing anyone here of murder." And if he were, Bianca wouldn't be the one he'd target with his allegations.

"If you were, the accusation wouldn't go far. I was out of town at Westside Medical Center the day Mr. McGraw died. I didn't hear about his death until I returned home," Bianca answered.

"Can I have the phone number to verify that?"

"Of course."

"Did anyone else in the family know Mr. McGraw was working for you?"

Bianca hesitated, her eyes straying to the chair where Miranda sat. The silence stretched for a moment too long. Then Miranda spoke, her voice calm. "I knew. And I don't have an alibi. I was here alone the night he died. My father and Aunt Winnie were both at a charity auction."

"You don't need an alibi. No one would ever suspect you of such a horrible thing!" Portia shot Mick a look filled with worry and frustration, but there was nothing he could say to ease her concern. His investigation had led him to her family. He'd follow it through until he found the answers he sought.

"I think we're at a dead end, Detective." Ronald moved toward the door. "Let us know if there's anything else we can do to help."

As dismissals went, this one wasn't subtle, but Mick had learned what he'd wanted to. Bianca and Miranda seemed forthcoming and willing to work with him. Ronald was a different story altogether. "Thank you for your time. I'll be in touch."

"Let me walk you to the door, Mick." Winnie

Blanchard stepped toward him, her hazel eyes asking questions he couldn't answer. At church they were acquaintances, maybe even friends. Here, Mick was a cop with a job to do.

"Aunt Winnie, you've been on your feet all day. I'll walk him out." Portia put a hand on her aunt's arm, her gaze on Mick. "I need to get something out of my car anyway."

"All right, but put your coat on. It's a bitter night."

"I will."

"Don't forget, Portia, we were planning to discuss your possible transfer to Blanchard Fabrics tonight. I'll expect to speak with you when I get home." Ronald's tone held a hard edge Mick couldn't ignore. He studied the other man, saw that he watched his daughter with a mixture of frustration and confusion, as if there were something about her he just couldn't understand.

And maybe that was the case. Portia did stand out from the rest of Ronald's daughters, her style alone separating her from her casually sophisticated sisters.

"Of course, Father." Portia's words were stilted, her expression blank, and Mick felt something stir in his chest, a need to step in, to offer protection. Though from what he didn't know.

He pushed the door open, held it as Portia proceeded him into the foyer, catching a whiff of sunshine and flowers as she passed. "Do you really need to get something from your car?"

"My cell phone. Though I suppose it could have waited until morning."

"But what you have to say to me can't wait?"

"Something like that." She smiled, relaxing for the first time since they'd walked into the house, her dark curls bouncing as she stepped outside.

Beyond the soft glow of the porch light the world was pitch-black, the moon and stars hidden behind thick clouds, the roar of the ocean a rumbling backdrop to the still night. What had it been like to grow up here, so close to the pounding fury of the ocean and the stunning beauty of cliffs? Mick supposed the experience would have been different for each of the six sisters, though he had a feeling that for Portia it hadn't always been a good one. He reached toward her, pulling her coat closed. "You need to button up. It's freezing out here."

"I'm okay." She wrapped her arms around her waist, holding the coat closed and emphasizing a too-thin frame. Had she been ill? Or was she one of those women that thought thinner was better?

And why did he even care? He raked a hand through his hair and tried to refocus his attention. "So, do you want to tell me why we're out here?"

"I want to know if you really believe my sisters are murderers."

"I don't believe anything…yet."

"Come on, Mick, we both know that's not true. You've got suspicions. I want to know what they are."

"I think Garrett McGraw's murder has something to do with your family."

"But—"

"But I don't think any of your sisters are involved."

"That doesn't leave many other possibilities."

"No. It doesn't."

Which meant, Portia thought, that Mick either suspected her father or her aunt. Since she couldn't imagine anyone believing that Aunt Winnie was a murderer, she had to assume he was going after her father. Should she bring it up? Would he? Before she could make up her mind, Mick spoke, his words doing nothing to put her at ease. "Your father has the most to lose if something happens to Blanchard Fabrics."

"That doesn't mean he'd kill to protect it."

"I hope you're right."

"I am." But even as she said it, Portia doubted her own words, her own belief in her father. If, as she suspected, he'd lied about her mother's death to keep Trudy Blanchard away from her children for almost twenty-three years, what else might he lie about? What else might he be capable of? Her heart beat hard with what she was thinking and Portia stepped back toward the door. "I'd better get back inside."

She didn't wait for Mick to respond, just shoved the door open and fled inside.

Mick waited until the door clicked shut, then headed to his SUV. Portia's loyalty to her family was something he admired, but it wouldn't keep him from doing his job. McGraw had been murdered. Mick might have lost his respect for the man who had been a childhood friend and, later, a fellow Portland police officer, but he couldn't allow that to influence his desire to solve the case. Especially since Mick had been partially responsible for McGraw's dismissal from the force years ago. If he'd known then...

He wouldn't have done things any differently. What happened was a result of McGraw's failures and sins, not Mick's, yet somehow he still felt responsible. The wind howled, tugging at Mick's leather jacket and urging him into the car and away from Blanchard Manor and his own dark memories. He couldn't change the past, wouldn't hurry the future. It was time to go home, to sit in front of a fire, maybe roast marshmallows with his six-year-old daughter Kaitlyn.

He glanced back at the house as he pulled onto Bay View Drive. Lights were blazing from all three levels, but still it seemed a lonely place and once again he was struck by the difference between Portia and the environment she'd grown up in. When he'd first seen her on the ice, he'd thought her to be carefree and exuberant. That had changed when she'd walked into Blanchard Manor. All her vitality had drained away, replaced by a quiet somberness that didn't match her bright clothing, or the vibrancy in her eyes. Had being around her father caused the change? Or was it the house itself, the staid, museum-like decor that had drained her?

And why had he even noticed or cared? It had been three years since his wife Rebecca had died in a plane crash. In that time, he'd created a life for himself and his daughter. A life that didn't include women. At least not women younger than Mick's mother. Now was definitely not time to change that. Not when he was responsible for investigating Stoneley's first murder in thirty years. And not when the woman in question was the daughter of Mick's prime suspect.

THREE

Portia watched the sunrise from the balcony off her room. French doors open, icy air seeping through her pajamas, she stood in awe as dawn painted the sky with vivid pinks and golds. For just this moment, she was exactly where she wanted to be, doing exactly what she wanted to do, no one hanging over her shoulder questioning her choices. She supposed that was the hardest part of belonging to a large family—always having people watching her, judging her actions.

If she were a different kind of person, what her sister, her aunt, even her father thought wouldn't matter quite so much. But she wasn't and it did. Which was why her conversation with Ronald the previous night had left her antsy and unhappy, his insistence that her New York City lifestyle was a mistake making her question her certainty about where she should be. Where God wanted her to be.

After all, wasn't that the point—to be where He wanted, doing what He wanted her to do, whatever that might be?

"And therein lies the problem. I have no idea what You want, God. I thought I did, but lately I'm just not sure."

"Talking to yourself again?" Rissa peeked in the room, her hair curling wildly around a makeup-free face.

"Talking to God." Portia threw herself down on the bed. "I don't think He's listening."

"Hmmm."

"Hmmm, what?"

"Hmmm, you had a nice long chat with Daddy dearest last night and now you're upset. Why am I not surprised?"

"Because you know Father never gives up once he sets his mind to something and he's set his mind to getting me to work for Blanchard Fabrics."

"Portia, he'd have every one of us working at the company if he had his way. Why do you let it bother you so much?"

"I don't know." And she didn't, though she wished she could change it. "Maybe because I'm a twenty-six-year-old woman who's still hoping to make her father proud."

"Don't hold your breath waiting for that to happen." Rissa stretched and yawned. "Do you have big plans for today?"

Portia did. She planned to visit the Stoneley police department to find out if there'd been any more progress on the McGraw case. That was something Rissa didn't need to know, though. "I'm running errands for Aunt Winnie and picking up that horrid dress from Mr. Dugal."

"Not the Winter Fest dress?"

"I'm afraid so."

"I thought you'd been saved that…honor."

"You mean humiliation."

"Hey, I wore it my senior year of high school. It wasn't that bad."

"Riding in a horse-drawn carriage, dressed like a winter princess is fine when you're seventeen. It's not fine when you're my age."

"*Our* age. So, say no."

"I tried, but Mr. Dugal takes a lot of pride in making sure every woman in Stoneley gets the opportunity. Apparently, he's decided it's my turn."

"And you didn't want to hurt his feelings so you said yes."

"Actually, Aunt Winnie accepted for me. She thought it might cheer me up. I didn't want to hurt *her* feelings."

"In that case, I forgive you for being a push over. And at least you won't go down in history as the oldest Winter Fest princess. Wasn't Jenny Wilcomb sixty-five?" Rissa yawned again, her eyes shadowed with fatigue.

"Forty, but thanks for trying to make me feel better. Now, stop yawning. You're making me tired."

"Sorry. I didn't sleep well last night."

"Me, neither."

"I doubt anyone did. We were probably all worrying about the same thing." Rissa dropped down onto the bed and threw her arm over her eyes. "Mother."

"And Garrett McGraw."

"And how much Father really knows about all of this."

"I think he knows a lot." Portia expected Rissa to agree and was surprised when her twin turned to face her. They were eye to eye, just inches apart the way they had been so many times when they were children and had something important to discuss.

"If he did, I don't want to know."

"How can you not?"

"Because if he's lied all this time, that means he's kept us from knowing our mother. I don't think I can handle that."

"You're one of the strongest people I know, Rissa. Of course you can handle it."

"I'm glad someone has faith in me." She pushed up

from the bed. "I think I'm going to hide out in my room today. I'll see you at the parade tonight."

"Hide out? Are you okay?" Worry brought Portia to her feet.

"Yeah, just working on my new play." Rissa pushed open the door and stepped out into the dark hall, her expression hidden by shadows. "Another week or two and I should have it done."

"I thought you were here for a vacation."

"I'm here for Aunt Winnie. And for you."

And if it weren't for them, Rissa wouldn't have come at all. She didn't say the words, but Portia knew the truth. In recent years it had been she, not Rissa, who'd pushed the idea of returning to Stoneley for Winter Fest. Next year, Rissa might not return at all. The thought made Portia sadder than it should have, and she smiled, trying to hide her feelings. "We know. And we appreciate it. Now, go get your work done, or you'll be blaming me when you fall behind schedule."

Portia watched Rissa disappear into her room, then closed her own door. Though the twins had always been in sync, Portia's affection for the town she'd grown up in had never made sense to Rissa. As far as she was concerned, they were well rid of Blanchard Manor and of Stoneley.

And maybe she was right.

But driving through the town, visiting the places she'd loved so much as a child, always felt like a homecoming in a way returning to New York never did.

Portia sighed and shook her head, grabbing clothes and a handful of jewelry. She needed to get out of the house, get some fresh air, not sit around moping about things she couldn't change.

Twenty minutes later, she was on her way, driving the vintage VW Bug she'd bought a few years ago, the scent of her aunt's homemade cookies and fudge wafting through the vehicle and making her stomach growl. She thought about snagging one of the oatmeal raisin cookies she'd seen Winnie pack, but the Winter Fest parade committee consisted of several women who weren't above counting cookies to make sure each volunteer had brought the proper number of snacks. If Winnie's offering was off by a cookie or two, she'd be the talk of the committee for months.

Maybe Portia would stop by Beaumont Beanery instead. Coffee and a Danish would go a long way toward waking her up. The thought cheered her and she hummed along with the radio, the lightening sky and crisp white clouds that sprinkled it making up for the long, restless night she'd had.

Today would be a better day than yesterday. A better day than the day before. As a matter of fact, Portia planned to make this the best day of the new year. She was still thinking that as the engine stalled and died.

Mick was running late. Ten minutes late, to be exact, the constant ringing of his cell phone reminding him again and again that he had twenty eleventh- and twelfth-graders waiting at the church for his arrival. He grabbed the phone, answering it for the fifth time in as many minutes. "Campbell here."

"You know you're supposed to be at the church." Roy Marcell, chief of police, good friend and co-leader of the church's youth group sounded as irritated as Mick felt.

"Yeah, I know."

"Just thought I'd make sure."

"You and ten other people. It's been a rough morning."

"Katie have trouble getting out of bed?"

"No, she had trouble finding matching shoes."

"Yeah, I remember those days. So, what's your ETA?"

"Ten minutes. Sooner if you've got coffee."

"You're in luck, so get here fast. The bus'll be here in fifteen."

"Right." Mick tossed the phone onto the passenger seat and rubbed the ache in his neck. When he'd volunteered to chaperone the youth group's ice-fishing trip, he hadn't planned to be heading a murder investigation at the same time. Five hours wasn't much time to lose, but it felt like too much when McGraw's widow and children were waiting for answers regarding his death.

He grimaced, rounded a curve in the road and braked hard as a neon-green Volkswagen Beetle appeared in front of him. The SUV fishtailed, but held the road as Mick maneuvered to the shoulder, his heart pounding with adrenaline.

He swung open the door and strode toward the car, watching as a woman stepped out. "Need some help?"

"It died on me. I think I'll need a tow." The voice was familiar, and Mick took in the delicate features, black curly hair and dark eyes. It could have been either of the twins, but somehow Mick knew it was Portia. Maybe it was the clothes—dark pants paired with a multi-colored coat—or maybe it was the tilt of her chin, the hint of laughter in her eyes. Whatever the case, he had no doubt which twin he was speaking to.

"You're out and about early."

"I could say the same about you, Detective."

"Mick, remember? Have you tried to start the car up since it stalled?"

"Not yet."

"Mind if I try?"

"Go ahead." She passed him the keys, her hands encased in fuzzy pink mittens that Kaitlyn would have loved. Somehow on Portia they worked, the quirky fabric adding to her unique style.

"Nice mittens."

"You're the first person over ten years old to say so."

"Yeah? Well, don't let it get around. I wouldn't want to ruin my tough-cop reputation." He slid into the Bug, the sound of her laughter following him and making him want to turn and watch the amusement playing out on her face.

But he didn't have the time, and not just because he was running late. A woman like Portia would need lots of attention. More than a man with a six-year-old daughter could give. Though Mick had to admit, he might be tempted to try if she didn't live a few hundred miles away. Being married to Rebecca had taught him an important lesson. A relationship with a woman who traveled more than she was home didn't work for him. He doubted a long-distance relationship would be any different.

He turned the key in the ignition, heard a quiet click and knew he was about to add a few more minutes to his ETA. "Looks like it's not budging. Where were you headed?"

"Town hall. Aunt Winnie asked me to drop off a few things for the parade tonight."

"Go ahead and put them in my truck while I call for a tow."

She looked like she was going to argue, so Mick pulled a bag of cookie-filled containers from the back seat of the Bug and handed it her. "I've got a bunch of teenagers waiting for me to chaperone their ice-fishing trip. If I don't give you a ride, I'll have to stay here and wait until the tow truck arrives. Let's save some time and do things my way."

To Mick's surprise, Portia gave in gracefully, grabbing the bag and carrying it to the SUV. Less than five minutes later, the Bug was safely on the shoulder of the road and they were on the way to Town Hall, the interior of the SUV filled with the scent of chocolate and something else—a flowery, feminine scent that Mick thought must be Portia's shampoo.

She glanced at him and smiled, her eyes shadowed and dark. "Thanks for the lift. I hope your ice-fishing crew won't leave without you."

"Seeing as how I'm one of the youth group leaders, I don't think I have much to worry about in that regard. Besides, Unity Christian isn't far from Town Hall. I'll only be a few minutes late."

"You're a youth group leader?" She turned toward him, tiny bells on her earrings jingling as she moved.

"Does that surprise you?"

"Maybe. I guess I didn't picture you as the church-going, youth-group-leading type."

Before Mick could ask what type she *had* pictured him as, she shifted in her seat, her hands clenched in her lap, her shoulders tense. "I was planning to come to the station to see you this morning. Since you're not going to be there, do you think we can talk now?"

"Sure."

"What you said about my father last night is…disturbing."

"I imagine it is, but I can't change the facts. Your father has a reputation to uphold and a company to protect.

That company is your family's bread and butter. Without it, your father can't maintain the lifestyle he's cultivated. Men have killed for less."

"I know, but I don't think my father would. He may be difficult at times, but he's no murderer."

"I don't doubt your sincerity in saying that, but I've got to check out the facts and find out the truth for myself." He pulled up in front of Town Hall and turned to face her.

She frowned, her eyes a deep brown that reminded Mick of milk chocolate and Valentines. He had the urge to lean forward, cup her cheek with his hand, see if her skin was as smooth and silky as it felt. And that was bad news.

He'd have to be careful around Portia. Really careful. Otherwise, he might find himself getting more involved than he intended.

"So you're going to keep investigating my family." She sounded tired and defeated, and Mick was surprised at how much that bothered him.

"I'm going to keep following my leads. Right now, they all head in that direction. By tomorrow, things might change."

"That's nice of you to say, Mick, but I don't think you really believe it."

He didn't, though he *was* checking out other possibilities. McGraw hadn't been a cop for long, but there was no doubt he'd made enemies while he was one.

Mick considered telling Portia as much, but for the sake of McGraw's family, he didn't. Bringing up the past would do no good, unless the past proved to be connected to the case. "Tomorrow is a new day. Anything is possible. That's something I *do* believe."

"A new day. Yeah, well, I hope it'll be better than the last few." Portia pushed the door open, anxious to get away, but Mick snagged her hand before she could retreat, his blue eyes searching hers.

"Has it really been that bad?" He brushed a strand of hair from her cheek, his fingers lingering there for a moment.

Portia blinked, surprised by his touch, by his words, by the concern she saw in his eyes. Did he really care that much about a woman he barely knew? If so, how would he act toward someone he loved?

Just thinking the question made her uncomfortable, and she tugged her hand away, reaching over the seat for the bag of baked goods. "No, not that bad. Just…" What? Discouraging? Disheartening? "Difficult. I used to think I understood our family. Now, I'm not sure it's anything like what I believed. And that's hard."

"You're talking about the new information regarding your mother."

It wasn't a question, but she answered anyway. "What else? But there are other things, too. It's hard not to worry and wonder when so much of what's happening is out of my control."

"I don't blame you for that, but worry never changes anything."

"My head knows that. My heart isn't convinced."

He watched her for a moment, then smiled, a slow, easy curve of his lips that made Portia's heart leap and her stomach tumble and twist.

"Tell you what, why don't we make a deal? I'll keep you updated on the case. You relax and stop worrying."

Did he really think it was that easy? "How about I promise to try not to worry?"

"Good enough. Here's my card. Call me if you have any questions or concerns."

Portia took the card, tucked it into her coat pocket and tried to get out of the SUV gracefully. As usual, her efforts fell short. Her boot caught on the edge of the door and she tumbled forward, nearly losing her grip on the bag and her purse.

"Careful." Mick grabbed her shoulder and pulled her back. "You destroy the stuff your aunt baked and you'll be the talk of the parade committee for the next ten years."

"I was thinking something similar, earlier. What is this? Three saves? Four?"

"Three, but who's counting?"

"Certainly not you."

Mick laughed and shook his head. "You'd better get that stuff inside. See you around."

He drove off as Portia stepped into Town Hall, and she told herself she was glad to be away from him. And she was. Mick wasn't the type of man that appealed to Portia. She liked a more scholarly type.

You mean more boring and less exciting.

The words whispered through her mind, mocking her as she dropped off the baked goods. It was true, she tended to date men who were predictable, stable, easy to understand. That didn't mean they were boring. Or maybe it did. But that was the way Portia liked it. She'd spent her childhood around men who were often unpredictable and moody. No way did she plan to repeat that pattern as an adult. Still, there was something about Mick she couldn't ignore. A vitality and energy that appealed to her, an honesty that spoke to the deepest part of her soul.

And there was something else.

It had taken Tad six months to figure out that one of the twins was left-handed, the other right-handed. Even after that, he'd often confused Portia and Rissa. Mick, on the other hand, had seen them together once, yet somehow he'd known which twin Portia was. She found that to be both interesting and alarming.

Portia rubbed a finger against the ache behind her right eye and shoved thoughts of Mick to the back of her mind. The day had just begun and she already had a headache. That didn't bode well for the remainder of the morning, let alone the afternoon and evening. She wanted to go back to the moment before the Bug had died, recapture the sense of excitement, of renewal. More than anything, she wanted to believe this really was going to be the best day of the new year and that all the days that followed would be better than the ones that had preceded her trip to Stoneley. Somehow, though, Portia doubted they would be. Unless she missed her guess, clouds were on the horizon—dark and foreboding—and no matter how much she might want to outrace the storm, she had a horrible feeling that it was only a matter of time before it caught up with her.

FOUR

Five hours later, Portia had a working car and a four-Tylenol headache. According to the mechanic who'd towed and fixed the Bug, her vehicle was in good shape. Now she just needed her head to follow suit. A few hours of quiet would go a long way to making that happen and she was relieved to see that the Manor's seven-bay garage was nearly empty.

Even Rissa's car was missing. Which meant either that her writing wasn't going well, or she couldn't bear another moment in the house. It was for the best. Portia had never been able to hide her feelings from her twin, and she had no desire to have to explain her conversation with Mick, or discuss his suspicions about their father. For now, she'd be content to keep the information to herself.

Briny air enveloped her as she hurried toward the house, the thick, salty scent of the ocean sweeping in from the cliffs. Watery sunlight filtered through the clouds, speckling the ground with gold, the trees with vibrant color. Portia's fingers itched for a paintbrush, the urge to capture the shift of light and shadow easing the pounding pain in her head. For the first time in months, Portia felt the urge to grab her easel and brushes and paint.

She hurried inside, started up the stairs, heard a soft wail from somewhere above and knew that painting was not in her near future.

"Aunt Winnie? Miranda?"

Heels tapped against the hardwood floor. A door slammed.

"Thank goodness you're home!" Sonya, the Blanchard housekeeper, appeared at the top of the stairs, the panicked expression on her face sending Portia racing toward her.

"What is it? What's happened?"

"You're grandfather. He…" Her voice trailed off as if she couldn't bear to continue.

"Is he all right?" Portia raced up the stairs, her heart pounding, her mind filled with a million possibilities, all thoughts of headaches and painting gone. An Alzheimer's patient, Howard Blanchard's health had been declining for years, but in the past few months there had been an even more drastic change.

Sonya shook her head, her dark eyes flashing. "He attacked Alannah. Put his hands around her throat and nearly strangled her."

"Strangled her? He can barely get up out of bed." Portia started up the stairs that led to her grandfather's third-floor suite.

"That's what we all thought, but I'm telling you, somehow he had enough strength to grab Alannah by the throat."

"Is she all right?"

"It's hard to tell with that one. She's in your father's office, now, threatening to call the police."

The police? That was the last thing they needed. "I'll talk to her."

"Someone better. You're grandfather is sick. Not a criminal." Her defense of Howard was a surprise. The tension between the housekeeper and her employer was something Portia and Rissa had often discussed. Neither knew the cause, they only knew it had always been there. Sonya's urge to protect Howard could only mean the housekeeper thought he was nearing the end.

Portia's heart beat faster at the thought and she put a hand on Sonya's arm, hoping the gesture would calm them both. "I'm sure Alannah understands that."

At least, she hoped she did. Her father's latest girl-friend was hard to read. That she was self-absorbed went without saying. Whether or not she was spiteful remained to be seen.

Portia hurried down the hall to her father's office. Sobs and jumbled words drifted through the door, and she knocked, then pushed it open. Alannah sat at Ronald's desk, clutching the phone to her ear and dabbing at her eyes with a tissue.

She met Portia's eyes, gestured for her to enter the room and continued speaking. "I'm telling you, he's dangerous. He had his hands around my throat. He could have killed me."

Portia was tempted to grab the phone and tell who-ever was on the other end of the line that Howard was too feeble to be dangerous, but Alannah was upset enough without her interference.

Instead, she took a seat in the chair across the desk from the other woman and waited.

"Of course I understand his condition, Ronald. You've told me about it often enough." Alannah sniffed, grabbed another tissue from a box on Ronald's desk. "I know. I know. Yes, I'll be there. Give me another half hour."

She hung up the phone, shot Portia an irritated look. "I suppose you're here to explain the intricacies of your grandfather's illness just like everyone else."

"I'm here to make sure you're okay." Making sure she didn't call the police was secondary to that, though Portia hoped she could manage it.

Alannah brushed strands of red hair away from her forehead, tucking them back into her chignon. "*Okay?* I just paid big bucks to have my hair styled. Now it's ruined."

"Loose chignons are in."

"If I'd wanted it loose, I would have asked the stylist for loose." Alannah's aquamarine eyes shimmered with unshed tears, but Portia suspected they were more from anger than fear.

"I know what happened must have been awful, but Grandfather—"

"Is sick and doesn't know any better. Miranda, Winnie and your father all said the same. I think I'm smart enough to get it."

"I know you are. I didn't mean to imply differently."

Alannah sighed and nodded. "Of course you didn't. I'm just upset. Whether your family wants to admit it or not, Howard has become dangerous." As she spoke, she stood, a diamond brooch winking in the light as she moved. Portia recognized the intricate pattern and Victorian setting. Howard had shown her the piece when she was a child. He'd told the story repeatedly about how his wife Ethel had fallen in love with it, how he'd purchased it from an antique dealer for their tenth anniversary.

"Is that my grandmother's brooch?" Before she could think better of it, the question escaped.

Alannah shot her a dark look, her hand hovering over the beautiful piece. "Yes. And before you accuse me of stealing it, Ronald told me I could wear it to the hospital fundraiser this afternoon."

"I wasn't going to accuse you of anything. I just wondered where you'd gotten it."

"From your grandfather's room. Your father was supposed to bring it by my place last night and forgot. I'd planned my entire outfit around the piece. I certainly couldn't go without it."

"No, of course you couldn't." Portia hoped Alannah didn't notice the sarcasm in her voice.

Alannah nodded. "I knew you'd understand. You're an artist, after all. Your father wasn't quite as understanding. He told me if I really felt the need to wear it, I'd have to come get it myself."

"That's why you were in Grandfather's room?"

"Yes. Ronald assured me it wouldn't be a problem, but your grandfather saw me pin the brooch on and," she paused, touching the skin on her neck. "Well, you know what happened next."

"Father should have explained that the brooch was his mother's. Grandfather gave it to her for their anniversary one year."

"Maybe he should have told me, but the fact that the piece is special to Howard doesn't excuse his behavior."

"It doesn't, but Grandfather didn't mean any harm. I hope you know that."

"Your grandfather tried to *strangle* me. If that's not trying to harm, I don't know what is. I'm sure the police would agree." She stood, straightened her slim-fitting skirt and started toward the door.

Police. The word, idle threat or not, was enough to bring Portia to her feet. "You're not planning to call them, are you?"

"Someone needs to make sure this doesn't happen again. If that person has to be me, so be it."

"Alannah—"

"I know you mean well, Portia, but I'm too upset to discuss this any longer. Besides, your father is waiting for me and I can't miss the luncheon." Alannah strode out of the room, closing the door firmly behind her.

"Great. Just great. One more thing to worry about." Portia sank down into the chair, her headache returning with a vengeance. Lately, it seemed every day brought a new set of troubles. Grandfather's attack on Alannah was bad enough, but if Alannah went to the police, news about what had happened would spread through town like wildfire.

Portia leaned back in the chair and stared up at the ceiling. Maybe she should call her father, tell him how determined Alannah was to contact the police, but what good would it do? Ronald had probably already tried to talk his girlfriend out of her plan. Maybe the best thing to do was nothing at all. Maybe, as Mick had told her, she should relax and stop worrying.

As if she could.

She sighed, her eyes scanning the room. It was her father's domain. One she'd rarely visited as a child and had seen even less of as an adult. It never seemed to change. The same leather chairs. The same polished wood desk. The same heavy drapes. All seemed exactly as they'd been the last time Portia had ventured into the office, the dark masculinity of it unappealing to her, but apparently exactly what her father preferred. And maybe that was the point. Ronald had never encouraged any of the Blanchard women to feel comfortable in his office.

She glanced around the room again, seeing it in a new

light—not a quiet retreat forged by a man whose home was overrun with young girls, but a hiding place for information he might not have wanted his daughters to find. Was it possible her father kept information about Mother there? If he'd lied about her death, if he'd known all along she was alive, would he have dared keep information about her in his home office? It didn't seem possible, but Portia had to know for sure. She pulled open the desk drawer, rifled through pencils, pens, paper clips and scraps of paper. The next drawer yielded just as little—current electric bill, water bill, credit card statement, phone bill. She paused, her hand on the last item, and then slowly pulled it from the pile. Most of the numbers listed were familiar, with the exception of three out-of-state area codes. She grabbed a piece of paper from her father's printer and jotted the numbers down, knowing she was violating his trust, but unable to turn away from the course she'd set. She was just returning the phone bill when the door to the study flew open. Portia jumped, closing the drawer and trying to look less guilty than she felt.

"What are you doing in here?" The housekeeper stood in the doorway, nearly quivering with indignation. "You know your father doesn't like his things touched."

"I was just getting a piece of paper and a pencil." That was part of the truth anyway.

"It looks like you've got it, so you'd better come out of there."

"I'm coming." She slid the paper into her pocket and stepped past Sonya. "I think I'll go up and check on Grandfather."

"Howard's just fallen asleep. It's probably better to let him rest."

Portia stiffened at the commanding tone, but decided not to argue. Sonya had been part of the Blanchard household for more years than Portia had been alive. While she could sometimes be overbearing, she always meant well. "I'll go up later, then."

Sonya nodded, her dark eyes shrewd. "Were you able to talk some sense into Alannah?"

"I tried."

"Hmph. I knew she wouldn't see reason. A woman like that is only interested in what she can get out of any situation."

"What do you mean?"

"She's probably hoping your father will give her the brooch. Or take her on another one of those fancy trips they're always going on."

"Sometimes you're a real cynic, Sonya."

"And sometimes you're naive, but I try not to hold it against you. Now, go. I've got plenty to do without having you under my feet."

The words were the same ones Portia had been hearing since she was a child, and she smiled as she moved away. The papers rustled in her pocket, stealing the grin from her face.

Sonya thought her naive, and maybe at one time she had been. But not anymore. Snooping in her father's office proved she was just as cynical as the housekeeper. Maybe the last few months had affected her more than she'd thought. Or maybe, like her father and Tad, she simply wasn't the person she'd thought herself to be.

The thought wasn't a comfortable one, but she couldn't let it go as she downed three Tylenol, grabbed her easel and paints and headed out to the cliffs.

FIVE

Portia had always found comfort in painting, in the challenge of blending colors, of smoothing paint onto canvas, of trying her best to recreate the beauty of God's creation. Being back in Stoneley only added to that feeling. Even as the wind slashed through her coat and gloves, she found a quiet peace out on the cliffs. High above, a hawk screamed. Far below, waves crashed against rock. Life, even in the frigid winter months, continued in the thick growth of evergreens, the spindly yellow grass and the glossy black birds zipping from tree to tree.

Portia dabbed more paint onto the canvas, feeling better than she had in months. *This* was what she'd missed. The quiet throbbing pulse of nature. New York City had its own pulse—an exotic beat that had appealed to her for a while. In the end, it hadn't found its way into her soul the way Stoneley had.

"I knew I'd find you out here." Rissa's voice sounded above the crashing waves, and Portia turned to watch her sister hurry across the clearing.

"I was wondering when you'd show up. Thought you were going to hide out and work today."

"Delia, Juliet and I decided to go into town. The house was too…"

"Quiet?"

"*Claustrophobic* was more the word I was thinking." Rissa studied her. "You look happy."

"I've always loved painting here."

"You've always loved *here,* period." She stared out toward the horizon, her eyes covered by dark sunglasses. "I know you don't want to come back to New York."

"That's not true."

"It is." Rissa smiled, the expression so sad, Portia's own content mood disappeared.

"The truth is, I don't know what I want anymore." She rinsed her paintbrush. "I'm not like you. I don't have one dream, one goal, one passion. I wish I did. Then maybe my choices would be clearer."

"If it weren't for Father, would you come back to Stoneley?"

Would she? It was a question she'd been asking herself over and over again since Tad went back to his ex. "Maybe."

"'Maybe' is not an answer. 'Maybe' is just you sitting on the fence, letting life pass you by because you're too afraid of standing up for what you want."

"Rissa—"

"I'm sorry. I shouldn't have said that. You're the kind of person who never wants to disappoint the people you love. I understand that. I just hope you don't regret it one day." Rissa shrugged. "Anyway, Sonya asked me to track you down. Mr. Dugal called to remind you that you're to be at the parade a half hour early. That gives you less than an hour to get there."

"It's that late already?" Portia grabbed her supplies,

hoping Rissa couldn't see how deeply her words had cut. It was true that she didn't want to disappoint those she loved, but was that so wrong?

Only if in refusing to disappoint them you ignore God's leading.

The thought weaseled its way into her mind and she pushed it away. Of course she wanted to go wherever God led. She just needed to figure out where that was.

Later. When she didn't have so much going on, so many things to deal with, she'd sit down and look at her options. For now, she'd just take things a day at a time and pray that God would keep her from making too many mistakes.

An hour later, she realized that He'd allowed her to make at least one. The Winter Fest Princess costume had seemed harmless enough when she'd picked it up earlier in the day. Now that she was wearing it, she was sure it had its origins as a medieval torture device. The corset top pinched in at the waist and the brocade skirt weighed almost as much as Portia herself. The tiara dug into her scalp and made her uncontrollable curls stick out in a hundred different directions. Beautiful she was not, but a promise was a promise, and she somehow managed to stuff herself and ten layers of petticoats into the Bug.

As she'd expected, the parade route was cordoned off, parking close to the beginning of the route was impossible. Fifteen minutes after she'd arrived in town, she parallel-parked between two pickups on a street fifteen blocks from where she needed to be. She was already five minutes late. Mr. Dugal wouldn't be pleased.

The heavy, fur-lined cape slowed her pace, but she managed a semi-jog, her high-heeled boots slipping and sliding over icy patches.

"You look like Cinderella running from the ball." Mick's voice was a deep, warm and all too familiar surprise. "Only, no glass slippers."

"Glass? Please. I'm having enough trouble in these." As if to prove the point, her foot slipped and she slid sideways.

"Maybe if you slowed down…" He grabbed her elbow, the amusement in his gaze obvious.

"I can't slow down. The parade is going to start in fifteen minutes and I've got to be in it."

"Ah, the Winter Fest Princess. I'd almost forgotten that tradition."

"Forgotten?"

"I grew up here. Went to school with your sister, Miranda."

"Really? I'm surprised I don't remember you."

"You were probably still in pigtails when I left town." His gloved fingers cupped her arm, his shoulder brushing against Portia's as they walked, and she was absolutely certain that if she'd ever met him, she would have remembered him.

She swallowed hard, trying to force down fluttery nerves she had no business feeling. "My pigtail phase lasted a while. I still sport the style sometimes."

"Not tonight, though." He used his free hand to touch the curls that framed her face, his eyes dark blue in the evening light. "I have to say, I like the curls."

"Thanks." She needed to change the subject fast. The conversation felt way too personal. "I guess your ice fishing trip is over."

"It had to be. I'm on duty tonight."

"Too bad."

"Not really. I haven't been to a Winter Fest Parade in

years. I'd forgotten how many beautiful sights there were to see." His words, coupled with the appreciative gleam in his eyes, were a quiet caress that stole Portia's breath.

"Yeah, well, the local businesses really do go all out to make impressive floats."

Mick laughed and shook his head. "I'm making you uncomfortable. I'll stop. There is Mr. Dugal's carriage, so I guess I'll say goodbye for now."

"Thanks for escorting me. I hope you didn't go too far out of your way."

"Actually, I ended up exactly where I needed to be. There's something we need to discuss." He turned to face her, the hardness in his eyes warning that Portia wasn't going to like what he had to say. "Your grandfather's actions earlier today."

He knew. Somehow he'd already found out about the attack against Alannah.

"I can tell from your silence that you know exactly what I'm talking about. How about we meet after the parade?"

"Mick—"

"Mr. Dugal is heading this way and he doesn't look happy. So, as much as I'd like to get your version of what happened this afternoon, I think it had better wait."

"But—"

"Portia Blanchard, what is it you're waiting for? A written invitation? The parade is about to start." Mr. Dugal's voice carried over the sounds of music and laughter that filled the night, and Portia winced, knowing she had to hurry or risk the entire town knowing she'd been late. That would almost be as bad for Aunt Winnie's reputation as coming up a few cookies short in the snacks she'd provided. After all, despite Portia and her sisters' ages, the town regarded everything they did as a reflection of the woman who had raised them.

"All right, I'll meet you after the parade."

"I'll be at the end of the parade route. Until then, do your best not to worry about it."

Portia nodded, but couldn't speak past the lump in her throat. Alannah had actually gone to the police. Could things get any worse?

"Stop frowning. I can't have a sour-looking Winter Fest Princess riding in the parade." Mr. Dugal helped her up into the turn-of-the-century carriage, his stooped shoulders set against the winter chill, his frizzy white hair peeking from beneath a black top hat.

Behind the carriage, the high-school marching band practiced, trumpets blaring, drums pounding a jazzy beat. Beyond them floats created by local businesses waited—a wedding cake made of flowers, a snow family perched in front of a gingerbread house. Portia couldn't see the rest, but knew from past experience they'd all be just as elaborate and beautiful. The comfortable familiarity of it should have eased her tension, but Mick's words made relaxing difficult and enjoying the carriage ride almost impossible.

People waved and shouted greetings as the carriage lurched forward and the parade began. Portia did her best to smile and wave in true Winter Fest Princess fashion, though her insides were knotted up tight, her pulse racing. Had Alannah pressed charges? Would the police be at the Manor when Portia returned? What would happen to Grandfather? The questions circled in her mind. The trip down Main Street seemed to take an eternity, the two-mile trek feeling more like twenty. Portia wanted to hop out of the slow-moving carriage and run to the end of the parade route. Unfortunately, the entire route was lined with spectators. Many were people she knew. It was bad enough to contend for the position of oldest Winter Fest Princess; she didn't want to go down in history as the only princess to abandon her post.

Finally, Mr. Dugal pulled on to a side street and parked the carriage. "That's it, end of the road. You want me to bring you back up?"

"No, my car is actually closer to this end."

"Then I'll let you out here. Enjoy the rest of the evening."

"You, too." She climbed down from the carriage and watched until it turned a corner and disappeared from sight. The alley was dark, shadowed by buildings to either side. Portia had been here many times as a child, playing with friends who lived in one of the Queen Annes that lined the street.

She started toward the mouth of the alley, hoping Mick would be easy to find in the crowd. The sooner she spoke to him and cleared things up, the better. Though she wasn't sure talking would do any good if Alannah *had* pressed charges. Something shuffled in the darkness behind her, a whisper of a sound that shivered along Portia's spine and had her turning to peer into the blackness.

"Hello?" Nothing moved, and Portia almost convinced herself that the sound had been her imagination. Then it came again. More a rustle than a footfall. Shadows shifted, a strange realignment of blacks and grays that made Portia blink and step back.

"Is someone there?" She backed up again, moving as quickly as she could in the cumbersome dress, afraid to turn her back on whatever stood in the shadows.

And bumped into something solid and unyielding.

A hand landed on her shoulder, holding fast as she jumped and screamed. She tried to turn, felt her feet slip out from under her and screamed again as she was pulled up into hard arms.

She twisted, struggling against her assailant's hold, her fist aiming for whatever it could connect with, panic giving her strength, a prayer for help shouting through her mind.

Mick grabbed Portia's fist seconds before it made contact with his face. "Whoa. Two broken noses in a lifetime is two too many."

"Mick?" She pushed against his arms and he eased her back onto her feet, feeling the quick, frantic beat of her heart and the fine tremors in the muscles beneath his hands. "You scared me half to death."

"Were you expecting someone else?" He made his voice light, even as he scanned the alley and the shadowy blackness behind the buildings. Something had frightened Portia, and he didn't think it was his sudden appearance.

"No. I just…" She turned her head, not even trying to free herself from his grip as she surveyed the area behind her.

"You just what?"

"Nothing." She faced him again, shrugging her narrow shoulders.

"It's not 'nothing.' You're shaking."

"I thought I heard something over there in the shadows." She gestured to the back of the alley and Mick pulled a flashlight from his pocket and shone it in that direction.

There was nothing but brick and pavement, the area to either side the same.

"See? Nothing. Just a dark night and an overactive imagination." She laughed, the sound hollow.

"Maybe." Mick released Portia and stepped toward the place she'd indicated. Nine times out of ten a noise in the dark was nothing. It was the one time out of ten that Mick was worried about. "Tell you what, why don't you go out onto Main Street? I'll meet you there in a few minutes."

"What are you going to do?"

"I'm just going to check around. It can't hurt to take a closer look." He cupped her upper arm and tugged her toward the lights and noise of the Winter Fest Parade. The band had passed and a float meandered by, boasting a three-tiered wedding cake of flowers complete with pint-sized bride and groom who waved cheerfully from their place on the top layer. People milled about on the sidewalk, laughing and chatting with one another. A few feet away, a street vendor sold pretzels to a smiling family. The scene was reminiscent of Norman Rockwell at his finest—small-town life portrayed to perfection. Yet, Mick couldn't shake the feeling that something tragic had just been averted. "Stay here."

"But—"

"Stay. Here." He doubted the added emphasis would keep her from following, but he hoped for it anyway.

The ground in the alley was snow- and dirt-covered cobblestone. Mick searched it for clues that someone besides Portia had been there. He found hoofprints and footprints. More than one set. Mick would be hard-pressed to say which were fresh and which were from earlier in the day, maybe even the week. The ground was frozen, the thin layer of snow and slush over the cobblestone unable to melt even during the warmest time of the day.

The soft slide of boots on the ground and the swish of the heavy skirt Portia wore announced her presence.

Mick wasn't surprised that she'd returned. "I thought we agreed you were going to wait out on Main Street."

"I thought you might need my help." The words, coming from a woman almost a foot shorter and probably a hundred pounds lighter, made Mick smile.

"I appreciate your concern, but I told you to stay put."

"How could I do that and help at the same time?" She stepped close, her arm brushing against his as she peered into the darkness. He caught a whiff of her shampoo and the subtle, flowery scent that was uniquely Portia.

"Did you find anything?"

"Footprints and hoofprints, but nothing conclusive."

"Then maybe we can get out of here. This place is giving me the creeps."

"Sounds good to me." He flashed the light into the shadows once more, the nagging worry in his gut not dissipating despite the fact that he could find no proof that Portia hadn't been alone. "What do you say to a cup of coffee somewhere warm?"

"Coffee?" That sounded like a bad idea to Portia. A really bad one. Discussing Alannah's accusations was one thing. Doing it over a cup of coffee was another. "I don't know. I'm not really dressed for it."

"You look perfect to me."

Thank goodness the darkness hid the color staining Portia's cheeks. "What I mean is that Mr. Dugal won't be happy if I spill coffee on the dress."

"Did you bring a change of clothes?"

"In my car."

"So let's go get them. You can change at the police station and we can hit the Beanery after that."

"Mick—"

"I'm not asking for a lifetime commitment, Portia. I'm

asking you to have a cup of coffee with me while we discuss what your grandfather did this afternoon. It's either that or we stand out here and discuss it. I spent most of the day outside. I'm about ready for a little warmth." He cupped her elbow and led her out of the alley, neatly stopping any argument Portia might have made.

She told herself that it didn't matter. That it was only a cup of coffee. But it felt like something more, and despite the fact that Mick wasn't her type, Portia had the alarming feeling that he could do even more damage to her heart than Tad had.

SIX

It didn't take long to reach the Bug and just a little longer to maneuver herself into it. She tried to shove the skirt out of the way so she could shut the door, but the bulky petticoats refused to cooperate. Exasperated, she looked up at Mick, who watched with undisguised amusement. "This isn't as easy as it looks."

"Need some help?"

"Not unless you have a pair of scissors and are willing to risk Mr. Dugal's wrath." She dropped the skirt and leaned her head back against the seat.

"No scissors, and I definitely don't want to risk Mr. Dugal's anger." He leaned down and tucked the skirt around her legs, his face so close to hers she could see the razor stubble on his chin and the specks of silver in his eyes. He looked handsome, rugged and much more appealing than Portia was comfortable with.

His hands stopped on either side of her knees, his gaze touching her hair, her cheeks, her lips. "You really do look like a fairy-tale princess tonight."

"As opposed to the clumsy, ditzy artist I looked like last night?" She tried for a light, funny tone and thought she mostly succeeded.

"No. As opposed to the exuberant free spirit I met last night." He stared into her eyes, as if searching for a truth even Portia didn't know. Finally, he backed up. "I'll meet you at the station."

She nodded, afraid to speak in case her voice sounded as breathless as she felt.

The police station was mostly deserted, the silent halls and darkened rooms eerie. Mick closed Portia into his office and stood guard outside the door while she changed. To her irritation, her hands were shaking as she packed the dress into the garment bag. Mick was just a man. A man who was *not* her type. All she had to do was keep that in mind while they had coffee together. If that wasn't enough to keep her heartbeat steady, then she just had to remember Tad and his pretty words and broken promises.

"Almost ready?" Mick called through the door.

Her heart leaped at his voice, a betrayal that Portia wasn't happy about.

"Hold on." She shoved her feet into her boots, yanked on her faux-fur coat and pulled the door open. "All set."

Mick smiled, seeming to take in everything about her with one glance. "From fairy-tale princess to epitome of professionalism. Do you have an outfit for every mood?"

Portia glanced down at the charcoal corduroys and emerald-green turtleneck she wore. "I hadn't thought about it, but I guess I do."

"That must make it easy for the people in your life to know how you're feeling." He took the dress bag from her hands and led her toward the exit.

Easy for the people in her life? She doubted any of them had ever noticed. She wasn't sure she'd noticed until Mick brought it up. Saying that to Mick would make her sound pitiful, so she decided to change the subject instead. "You said you spoke to Alannah."

"She caught me a few minutes after I got back from the fishing trip."

"What did she say?"

"Exactly what you're probably afraid she said." He pulled open the door of his SUV and gestured her inside. "She accused Howard of attempted murder."

"Murder? He can barely get out of bed."

"That may be so, but according to Alannah, Howard had his hands around her throat. I can see why she'd think he was trying to kill her."

"She wasn't hurt, was she?" She'd seemed fine when she walked out of Ronald's office, but maybe she'd had bruises Portia couldn't see.

"There wasn't a mark on her, but that doesn't mean she wasn't hurt. Emotionally, she's been through the ringer."

"I know. And I feel terrible about what happened, but she was wearing a brooch that belonged to my grandmother. Grandfather thought she was stealing it."

"That doesn't excuse what he did."

Mick parked at the Beanery and came around to open Portia's door.

"I know that. Of course, I know that. It's just…"

"Just what?"

She sighed, pulling her coat closed against the cold. "I love Grandfather. The thought of anything happening to him breaks my heart."

"Nothing is going to happen to him. Alannah won't be pressing charges, provided your family takes measures to make sure nothing like this happens again." His words weren't comforting. Alannah might not press charges, but the fact that she'd gone to the police filled Portia with a cold sense of dread she couldn't shake.

"You're worrying again. I thought we agreed you wouldn't." Mick's words pulled her from her thoughts.

"We agreed I'd try not to."

"That frown on your face says you're not trying very hard." Mick pushed open the door to the Beanery, the pungent scent of coffee offering the illusion of comfort and warmth.

But an illusion was all it was. All the coffee, all the bright lights and cheerful sounds in the world couldn't ease the chill that had settled deep in Portia's soul.

"It's difficult not to worry when so many things are going wrong."

"What things?" He put a hand on the small of her back, urging her to the table a waitress led them to.

"Do you even have to ask? A month ago, I learned my mother might be alive. Now, you're investigating my family. To top it off, Grandfather's Alzheimer's is getting worse."

"You keep forgetting that I'm investigating a murder, not your family." Mick gave the waitress his order, and Portia did the same, fiddling with a napkin on the table, avoiding Mick's intense gaze.

"It feels the same to me."

"I guess I can understand that." He placed a hand over hers, stilling its movement, his palm warm against her chilled skin. "Look, I hate to bring this up, but I told you I'd keep you updated on the case. There's something else I want to talk to you about before I go back on duty."

"What's that?"

"I've put some feelers out and started asking questions about Blanchard Fabrics. I want to know everything Garrett McGraw knew before he died."

"Because you think that something he knew about my family got him killed." She stared across the table at him, but could read nothing in his eyes.

"That's one of the possibilities. I'm following a few other leads."

"Like?"

He hesitated, then shook his head. "Nothing I'm willing to discuss right now." His gaze shifted to a point somewhere behind Portia. "Your sisters are looking for you."

She glanced over her shoulder, saw Bianca, Delia, Rissa and Juliet hovering in the coffeehouse doorway and waved them over, not sure if she was relieved or frustrated by the interruption. "It doesn't look like Miranda came with them."

"She doesn't get out much, does she? I don't think I've seen her more than once since I moved back to town."

"Less and less lately."

"Where have you been, Portia?" Delia called out from across the room. "We've been looking everywhere."

"Just getting changed."

"And having coffee." Rissa's gaze went from Portia to Mick and back again. "We were planning to get a pretzel and hot chocolate with you, but it can wait for another night."

"Don't let me keep you from it." Mick stood, his tall, broad frame dwarfing Portia's sisters. Tad had been as tall, but hadn't seemed to take up nearly as much space. "My break is over in five minutes, so I've got to head back out on patrol. Do you want me to give you a ride back to the station, or will one of your sisters?"

"I'll catch a ride with one of them, thanks."

"Great. You've got my card, call if anything comes up."

As soon as he stepped out of the coffeehouse, Rissa grabbed Portia's hand and pulled her to her feet. "You ditched us for a police detective. What's going on?"

"I didn't ditch you. We weren't suppose to meet until after the parade."

"The parade is over, Sis," Humor flashed in Delia's eyes. "I guess you were so wrapped up with your new guy you didn't notice."

"He's not my 'guy.'" But Portia couldn't stop the smile that hovered on her lips at her sister's teasing.

"No? It sure looked like the two of you were pretty cozy."

"We were sitting in a crowded coffeehouse. How cozy could we be?" Portia kept her voice light as she and her sisters stepped out into the frigid night air.

"Stop teasing her, Delia." Bianca linked an arm with Portia. "Ignore her, Portia. She's just jealous that you were off having coffee with a nice-looking guy while she was hanging out with her sisters."

"Nice-looking?" Mischief glinted in Delia's eyes. "Obviously, your relationship with Leo has warped your perspective. Mick is a little bit more than *nice*-looking. Right, Portia?"

"If I say yes, you'll be razzing me for the rest of the night."

"And if you say no, we'll do the same." Juliet smiled. "So why not just admit you find him attractive?"

"Fine. I find him attractive." And strong and determined and fun to be around. Which meant absolutely nothing. "But he's not my type."

Delia snorted. "Your problem is you don't know what your type is."

"We're getting off the subject here," Rissa broke in, probably hoping to forestall further discussion of Portia's choice in men. "Does Mick have any more information about Mr. McGraw's murder?"

"Not yet. He said he was researching Blanchard Fabrics."

"Hoping to uncover some skeletons in our closets, I suppose. There should be plenty to find."

"Don't be such a pessimist, Juliet. I doubt we've got anything to worry about hidden away." Bianca spoke with confidence and Portia wished she didn't have more bad news to share.

"Maybe not, but there is something that could be cause for concern. Alannah spoke to Mick about what happened this afternoon."

"You've got to be kidding me! Father needs to have a long talk with her." Rissa sounded outraged, and the rest of the sisters joined her, their voices rising and falling in complete harmony despite the differences between them.

Portia let the conversation wash over her, let herself relax into its rhythm. All around her, the night was alive with music and laughter, the air redolent with the sharp, clean scent of pine boughs and smoky wood fires. Her heart ached with the beauty of it and with the need to capture the moment, to seal the memory deep inside. Her sisters, the exquisiteness of Stoneley in February, the quiet, lilting melody of joy.

"You okay?" Rissa whispered in her ear, her hand squeezing Portia's in question and reassurance.

"Yes. Just enjoying the night."

And praying with all her heart that the peace of the moment would last.

SEVEN

"Daddy, wake up!"

Mick groaned, pulled the sheet over his head and tried to ignore his six-year-old daughter's plea. "Tell Grandmom she and Granddad can take you to church. I'm…" Not sick. What excuse would his daughter and his mother believe that would be good enough to buy him a few more hours of sleep?

"Michael Isaac Campbell, tell me that you are not trying to come up with an excuse to stay home from church." His mother's amused voice floated into the half-asleep fog Mick was still in.

"I would, but that would be a lie, and lying on Sunday could get me in big trouble."

"Lying any day will get you in trouble, Daddy. Honesty is always the best policesty," Kaitlyn said solemnly.

"Policy." He shoved the sheets off his face and frowned at his daughter. "You do know what happens to little girls who wake their fathers up, don't you?"

"They get ice cream?" Katie laughed, two strawberry-blonde braids bouncing against her shoulders.

"No, they get tickled." He pulled her up onto the bed and tickled her belly. "Were you good for Grandmom?"

"The best. Right?" She shot a hopeful look at Mick's mother, her freckled cheeks flushed.

"You're always the best." His mother hovered in the doorway, her trim figure encased in a stylish wool coat. "But I think we should discuss that later. After your father is dressed and ready to go. You do realize it's ten past nine, Mick?"

"I hit snooze one too many times. Late night."

"Well, you can't snooze anymore, Daddy, my Sunday school class is singing at the service today and we need to practice, so I've got to be there early."

"I'm moving, Katie. Give me fifteen minutes and I'll be ready to go."

"Good, 'cause I don't want to be late to practice. And guess what?"

"What?"

"Grandmom did my hair in braids so I'd look extra pretty today."

"It looks great, but you always look extra pretty." He kissed the top of her head and shooed her off the bed.

"You always say that."

"Because it's always true. Now get out of here so I can get ready."

"You won't go back to sleep?" She eyed him with suspicion, her blue eyes spearing into his, the freckles on her nose and cheeks standing out in stark contrast to her winter-pale skin.

"And miss hearing you sing? No way, not gonna happen. Now scoot."

"Okay, but if you don't come out soon, I'm going to come in and wake you up again." She hurried from the room, her pink coat a poofy cloud around her small frame, a denim skirt covered with pink embroidered flowers peeking out from beneath it. It was a new skirt, unless Mick missed his guess. And the fur-trimmed pink boots were new, too. They reminded him of Portia's fuzzy pink mittens. Obviously, she and Katie had something in common.

"Before you say anything, the boots and skirt were on sale." His mother's voice broke into his thoughts, and Mick smiled, shaking his head.

"So, of course, you had to buy them."

"I had three sons, Mick, be glad I saved my yen for pink and ruffles for my granddaughter." She leaned against the door jamb, her arms crossed over her chest, apparently in no hurry to leave.

"You know, it'll be easier for me to get up and get ready if you give me a little privacy."

"Privacy? After what I heard about you last night?" She smirked, her pale skin and freckles an older version of Katie's.

"The rumor mill sure works fast around here."

"So you *were* out with one of the Blanchard women."

"I was having coffee with Portia." He shoved aside the covers and stood. "Now that we've gotten that out of the way, can I get ready?"

"Sure, but I'll expect to hear more about her on the way to church."

"I was thinking of taking the SUV."

"Your father and I drove Katie all the way here. The least you can do is ride to church with us."

"Mom, you live three houses away."

"My point exactly. If we hadn't wanted to drive together, I would have walked Katie home. Now, get ready before you make us late."

Mick laughed and closed the door. He supposed he

could deal with ten minutes of his mother's curiosity. The fact was, he owed his parents a lot. They took care of Katie when he worked the occasional night shift, and sometimes watched her after school. Family was one of the reasons he'd come back to Stoneley. The most important one. Though, he had to admit, he'd missed the quiet pace of life and the tight-knit community, too. Funny that what had driven him away had been exactly what had drawn him back. If Rebecca had lived, he might have been content to stay in Portland, but after her death, the city had lost its appeal. This was where he belonged. Even if that meant being fodder for the gossip mill every time he spent a few minutes with a woman.

Half an hour later, Mick stood in the kitchen of Unity Christian Church, nursing a cup of coffee while he half-listened to Sigmund Jefferson explain why the police should investigate his neighbor's suspicious activity. "What d'ya think, Mick? Don't that seem odd?"

"That John and Reena were out until ten o'clock on a weeknight?"

"Three nights in a row. What's there to do in a place like Stoneley that late at night *three nights in a row?*"

"Bowling?"

"At their ages? No one over fifteen or younger than forty bothers with that bowling alley."

"Isn't the Y offering square-dancing lessons? Maybe they decided to take up a new hobby."

"Square dancing? You're a big-city investigator, you can't come up with something better than that?"

"Well—"

"You know what I'm thinkin'?" Sigmund leaned in, his gnarled beard and wrinkled face so close Mick could smell the mint gum he'd favored since he gave up smoking twenty years before.

"What?"

Sigmund glanced around the empty kitchen, peered out the open doorway into the hall, then whispered loudly enough to be heard in Timbuktu. "Drugs."

"Drugs?" Mick tried to wrap his mind around the fact that an eighty-five-year-old man was accusing his thirty-something neighbors of being involved in the drug trade. Fortunately, he was saved from commenting by Reverend Gregory Brown's entrance into the kitchen, the amusement in his eyes indicating that he'd heard at least part of the conversation.

"Good morning, Mick. Sigmund." He grabbed a cup, poured coffee. "I'm surprised you're both in here. The food is in Janet McPharlin's adult Sunday school class."

"Food?" Sigmund perked up, his rheumy brown eyes brightening.

"Peach and apple cobbler. Janet made it herself."

"Did she?" Sigmund straightened his spare frame, his eyes gleaming. "I haven't had a good peach cobbler since my Agatha passed. We'll talk later, Mick. I got some other ideas about what we were discussing."

"I'm sure you do." Mick mumbled the words as the older man disappeared around the corner.

Greg chuckled and took a sip of coffee. "You're chipper today."

"Long day yesterday, followed by a longer night."

"I heard the ice-fishing trip was a success."

"It was. The kids had a great time."

"I heard something else, too."

"Yeah?" If the reverend brought up Mick's coffee

with Portia, he might start thinking small-town life wasn't quite as amusing as it had seemed earlier.

"Rumor has it Howard Blanchard went crazy and attacked Alannah."

That was worse than more talk about Mick and Portia. If the press got hold of the information, it would be all over the papers by morning. "Rumors aren't always based on fact, Greg."

"Avoidance. I guess that answers my question about whether or not the rumors are true." He sighed and took another sip of coffee. "It's a shame. The family has already been through a lot."

"Which was why I'd hoped the information wouldn't get out."

"I'm not planning to spread it, if that's what you're worried about." Greg smiled. "I was hoping to nip it in the bud."

At this point that was all they *could* hope for.

Mick had tried assuaging Alannah's wounded pride. Maybe it was time to talk to Ronald. Unfortunately, that would have to wait for another place and time. Mick ran a hand over his jaw. His eyes were gritty from lack of sleep, his stomach hollow and empty. The lukewarm coffee wasn't working to wake him up, fill his belly or change his frustrated mood. So, maybe it was time for something else. He tossed the foam cup into the trash can. "I think I'll go see if Sigmund saved any of that cobbler."

"Better hurry. That guy may look scrawny, but he sure knows how to pack away food."

Mick nodded, but didn't hurry. It wasn't the cobbler he was after. Winnie Blanchard was a member of the Sunday school class. Maybe now was a good time to feel her out, see what she thought about Alannah's allegations and their potential impact on the family and company. Winnie's personality might be far removed from her brother's, but they both had a vested interest in Blanchard Fabrics and in the six girls they'd raised together. Where Ronald might shrug off the rumors, Winnie would work hard to stop them. Not for the sake of the company, but for the sake of her nieces.

Portia stood at the doorway to Winnie's Sunday school class and peered inside. If she waited another minute or two, the class would start and she could slip into a back seat unnoticed.

"Are we waiting for an invitation?" The words came from behind her, and Portia spun around, her heart racing as she met Mick's gaze.

He looked good—all hard angles and rough edges, the stubble on his chin only adding to his appeal. "Maybe I was waiting for you."

Dumb, dumb, dumb. Flirting with Mick was definitely on the list of things *not* to do.

He raised an eyebrow, a half smile curving his lips. "Then your wait is over. Here I am." He wrapped a hand around hers and tugged her to his side, his eyes scanning her winter-white dress and the pink heels she'd paired it with. "Nice outfit. I especially like the shoes." There was a hint of laughter in his voice and in his eyes, and Portia couldn't stop her own answering smile.

"I can get you a good deal on a matching pair."

"I doubt they'd have them in my size." His hand rested on her spine and he ushered her into the Sunday school class. "My daughter would love them, but she's a little young for spike heels."

Daughter? Portia's muscles tensed, her face heating, thoughts of Jasmine and Tad filling her with the same sick dread she'd felt the night before.

"Then maybe for your wife." She pulled away from his hand, putting as much distance as she could without making what she was doing obvious.

Of course, he noticed anyway, lifting an eyebrow in silent question.

"Rebecca died three years ago."

"I'm sorry."

"Thanks. It's been hard. Katie's at an age where she really misses having a mother."

"I understand how that is."

"I'm sure you do." He studied her face, his eyes the blue of a spring day—bright, clear and full of promise.

But Portia had seen those promises before, heard them, felt them flutter to life in her heart, only to have them die a quick and brutal death.

She wouldn't let that happen again, and tried to keep her voice neutral, her expression bland. "It was hard growing up without a mother, but I had my aunt. She did her best to fill that hole in my life."

"My mom is doing the same for Katie, but it's still difficult."

Portia expected him to continue, maybe make some attempt at setting up a meeting between his motherless daughter and the woman he must suppose would understand her plight. And Portia did understand, but she also knew that that understanding came with a price—her heart. As far as she was concerned, it had been broken enough for one lifetime. "Does your daughter enjoy spending time with your mother?"

"Are you kidding? Mom spoils her like crazy. Katie

spent the night with my parents and came home in a new outfit to wear at her performance this morning."

"Performance?"

"Her Sunday School class is singing during the service. Twenty kids all dressed up in their Sunday best. It should be cute."

It would also be heartbreaking, but Portia didn't say as much. "Which one will your daughter be?"

"I think I'll wait and see if you can spot her." He smiled, gestured to two seats at the back of the class. "You first."

She couldn't think of a polite way to refuse and sat where he'd suggested, her muscles tense, a throbbing ache in her chest reminding her of what she'd left behind in New York. She'd been so sure of her relationship with Jasmine, so confident that one day she'd officially be the young girl's stepmother. Now Jasmine was back with both parents, happy, loved. And Portia was alone.

She blinked back tears, refusing to give in to the sorrow that haunted her.

"I don't see Winnie. Didn't she come?" Mick slid down into the seat next to her, his long legs stretched out and crossed at the ankle. He looked relaxed and completely oblivious to Portia's rioting thoughts.

Which was just the way she wanted it. "No. Grandfather wasn't doing very well today, so she and Miranda stayed home to help the shift nurse. Our full-time nurse, Peg, needed a break."

"I don't see the rest of your family, either."

"They'll be here for the service."

"Your father, too?"

The conversation was heading somewhere, Portia just wasn't sure where. "He and Alannah both. Why?"

"I was hoping to speak with him and Winnie. Rumors are spreading about what happened yesterday. It might be best for them to take the offensive and explain the incident before the press makes it into something it's not."

Portia's heart sank, but she nodded. "I'll make sure they know."

And then she'd go speak with Alannah, tell her just how harmful her gossip might be to the family.

"Thanks. Do something else for me, will you?" He leaned toward her, his words soft, his eyes searching hers.

She felt breathless, flustered and irritated with herself for both. Mick was investigating a murder tied to her family. That alone made him off-limits. The fact that he had a daughter only made her more determined to keep her distance. "What's that?"

"Let Ronald and Winnie take care of Alannah."

"I planned to." Sort of.

"No, you didn't." He flashed her a grin, turning to face the front of the room as the teacher began to speak.

Portia tried to concentrate on the lesson, but her mind buzzed with thoughts and worries, her heart ached with what she'd lost and what she might soon lose. God knew what He was doing. Portia believed that. She only wished *she* had a clue.

EIGHT

Portia used her family as an excuse to hurry away from Mick after Sunday school. Cowardly, yes, but she had enough to worry about without adding a man into the mix. Her father, sisters and Alannah were already seated as she walked into the sanctuary. Peg, Grandfather's home-health-care nurse, huddled at the end of the pew, her pale prettiness set off by the royal-blue dress she wore. Portia smiled a greeting and squeezed in beside her, trying not to shoot an angry glance at Alannah as she did so. As much as she sympathized with her father's girl-friend, she couldn't understand how Alannah could have spread the story about what Howard had done. It seemed almost cruel in light of Howard's condition.

Portia would have to speak with her father. Of course, doing so would give him another opportunity to bring up the benefits of her working for Blanchard Fabrics. One lecture per visit was plenty. Maybe she'd talk to Aunt Winnie instead. Let her speak with Ronald about his girlfriend.

Which was as cowardly as running from Mick had been.

Portia rubbed her aching forehead and tried not to

think about what that said about her. Hadn't she always been the free spirit in the family? The fashion maverick? The one least likely to follow the crowd? Since when had she ever been afraid to go after what she wanted, or say what she meant?

Since forever. As much as Portia hated to admit it, Rissa was right. She *did* worry too much about what other people thought. Maybe that was the point of all the trouble she'd been through. Maybe she needed to learn to listen to God rather than all the other voices vying for her attention.

The service began and a line of children filed in. Brunettes, blondes and redheads in various sizes and shapes. Pudgy, thin, tall, short, wiggly and still. She knew she shouldn't look, but Portia found herself scanning each face, trying to find Mick's daughter. She imagined a child with wheat-colored hair and vivid blue eyes, spotted two girls with that coloring and was trying to decide which looked more like Mick when the kids walked up on stage, their feet pounding on the carpeted steps. Black and brown dress shoes on the boys. Patent leather on the girls. And one pair of bright pink boots decorated with fur trim.

Portia blinked, looked again. Yep. The kid was sporting pink boots, a denim skirt with pink flower embroidery and a fuzzy yellow sweater. Two chunky braids lay over her shoulders, wisps of strawberry-blond hair escaping them to curl around the little girl's freckled cheeks.

Mick's daughter. She had to be.

Portia glanced around the crowded church, saw Mick sitting at the end of one of the front pews. He turned his head, met her gaze and mouthed the words, "Nice shoes." She could see the laughter in his eyes, could almost feel it shivering along her spine.

Her stomach lurched, her heart leaped and she knew she was in serious trouble.

When church ended, she dashed for her car, not bothering to wait for her sisters or father. She knew she was running, but couldn't seem to stop herself. She almost made her escape. Almost.

"Portia!" Alannah called out from somewhere behind her and Portia turned, saw that her father, Alannah and Peg were striding toward her.

"You couldn't take five minutes to chat with your family before you ran out?" Ronald's tone rang with disapproval.

"Sorry. I figured we'd see each other at the Manor in a few minutes."

"Actually, your father made reservations for all of us at the Coastal Inn. We both thought it would be a nice way to celebrate having the family together." Alannah offered Portia a chilly smile.

"That sounds…" Horrible. Meals with Ronald were always formal, stuffy and filled with discussion of Blanchard Fabrics. "Nice, but I want to get home and relieve Miranda and Winnie."

"Why? It's not as if Dad needs either of them there. He's got a shift nurse with him and he probably won't even know who you are."

"I know that, Father, but I'm only here a few weeks out of the year. I'd like to spend part of that time with Grandfather. Who knows how many more years he's got left?"

"Who knows how many *I've* got left? But that doesn't seem to be a reason for you to spend more time with *me*."

For a moment Portia thought Ronald might really want to share a nice, homey meal with her. Then he ruined it by shaking his head and running a hand through his still-thick hair. "Look, Portia, I know you don't see the benefits of using your creativity at the company right now, but I really think you'll regret that in a few years. Come to lunch. We'll talk about it. I'm sure the salary you'll make is more than what you're getting out of that little store you own."

"We've already discussed it. I'd rather not cover the subject again. Not today, anyway. I really do want to get back to the Manor."

He looked as though he wanted to argue, but Alannah put a hand on his arm. "We've really got to go if we don't want to be late. The Inn won't hold our reservation."

"You're right." Ronald patted Alannah's hand. "I won't bother to keep insisting, Portia. Obviously, you've got other plans for this afternoon. Enjoy them."

Portia forced herself not to wince at his cold tone. "Thank you, I will. Enjoy your lunch."

"Since you're going back to the Manor, would you mind giving me a ride?" Peg spoke quietly, her cheeks pale pink. She'd been Howard's home-health-care nurse since he'd broken his hip four years earlier. In the years since, she'd become like a part of the family.

"Of course. I'd be happy to."

"Just because Portia wants to skip lunch doesn't mean you have to, Peg. You deserve an afternoon away after the rough week Dad's had." Ronald turned on the charm as easily as he turned on his icy coolness.

The color in Peg's cheeks deepened. "Howard *has* had a difficult week. An afternoon away would be nice."

"That settles it. We'll all go and enjoy a relaxing lunch while Portia mopes."

"I'm not—" But Ronald and the two women were moving away and there was no sense in continuing.

"You look like you lost your best friend." Mick strode across the parking lot, the boot-wearing little girl at his side, an older couple trailing along behind. Portia wanted to turn away, pretend she hadn't seen or heard him, but knew he'd know the truth.

"Just my sanity." She tried to smile, failed miserably and settled for digging her keys out of her purse.

"Want to talk about it?"

"It would take a lifetime to explain." She refused to meet his eyes, focusing her attention on his daughter instead, her heart aching as she looked into the little girl's face. "You must be Mick's daughter."

"I'm Katie."

"I'm Portia. It's a pleasure to meet you." Portia held out her hand and smiled when the little girl shook it.

"I like your name, but I like your shoes better." Katie's eyes were the same clear blue as her father's.

"Funny, your dad was admiring them, too. I told him I could get him a pair if he wanted."

Katie wrinkled her nose and giggled. "Daddy in pink shoes? That would be funny."

"It would be. Especially if they were pink heels, like mine. He'd probably be falling and tripping all day long."

"He'd have to be careful. Maybe shoes like mine would be better." She stuck out one pink boot.

"They're definitely cool. What do you think, Mick, boots or heels?" Portia met Mick's eyes, then looked away quickly. She needed to get out of the situation *now* before she became any more comfortable with Mick and his daughter.

"I think I'll stick with my boring black dress shoes." He put his hand on the small of Portia's back, urging her around to face the couple walking up behind him.

"Portia Blanchard, these are my parents, Debbie and Jack Campbell."

"It's nice to meet you."

"Nice to meet you, too, Portia." Debbie's eyes were like her son's and granddaughter's, vibrant and filled with life, her smile warm and welcoming. "Your aunt and I are in a Bible study together. She's told me so much about you and your sisters."

"I hope only good things."

"Of course. She's always talking about the art shop you have in New York. You teach, too, don't you?"

"Our store offers art and craft classes for kids."

"Really?" Katie cut in, nearly dancing with excitement. "I love art and I love doing crafts. Grandmom and I make things all the time."

"What kind of things?" Despite herself, despite knowing that getting involved in another child's life was a mistake, Portia couldn't help feeling drawn to the little girl.

"Jewelry mostly. I have lots of beads and stuff."

"Really? Making jewelry is one of my hobbies. I teach kids your age to make charm bracelets."

"Maybe you could—"

"No," Mick interrupted, a look of patient amusement on his face.

"But, Daddy—"

"Portia isn't here to teach. She's here to spend time with her family."

Katie looked disappointed, but didn't persist. "Well, maybe I could see some of the jewelry you've made?"

"Actually, I'm wearing a bracelet I made." Portia pushed up her coat sleeve and revealed the silver and peridot charm bracelet.

"That's beautiful." Katie leaned forward to examine the piece. "How'd you get the peridot to hang like that?"

"I'm surprised you know what gem this is. Most kids don't." Surprised. Impressed. *Worried.* Portia had been the same way as a kid—more interested in gems and settings, paint and canvases, than in dolls and games. It had made her an oddity in elementary school, a pariah in middle school and clueless in high school. That had been fine with her. She'd had five sisters at home to hang out and have fun with.

Mick's bright-eyed, freckle-faced artist was an only child.

But that wasn't Portia's business and she couldn't make it her concern. Not if she wanted to leave town with her heart intact.

"I know a lot about gems. Daddy bought me books and everything. Someday I'm going to be a famous jewelry designer," Katie spoke with breathless enthusiasm.

"You're lucky to have a dad who is helping you learn about what you love."

"I know, but Daddy doesn't know much about jewelry. Not like you. I bet you could teach me so much. Like how—"

"Kaitlyn Rose Campbell, didn't I just tell you that Portia wasn't here to teach classes on jewelry making?"

"It's okay, Mick. I don't mind." Portia smiled up at Mick and his breath caught in his lungs. She looked beautiful. Worse, her kindness toward his daughter put him in serious danger of rethinking his no-long-distance-relationships policy.

"Maybe not, but we all need time away from our jobs sometimes. Katie needs to respect that. Right, Katie?"

"Yes, Daddy." His daughter was still studying

Portia's bracelet, her face enraptured. In this one way, she was absolutely her mother's daughter. Rebecca's love for fine gems had led her around the globe. Her jewelry store in Portland had been up-and-coming, a place people came from miles around to shop at. She'd died when the small plane she'd hired to fly her to New York for a jewelry show had crashed. Some days Mick found comfort in knowing she'd died doing what she'd loved.

"Invite Portia to lunch, Mick." His mother's stage whisper was as subtle as Portia and Katie's clothing styles.

"Mom—"

"Fine, then, I'll do it. Portia, would you like to join us for lunch? We're having clam chowder and home-made rolls."

"I wish I could, Mrs. Campbell, but my grandfather hasn't been doing very well and I need to get home." Portia's cheeks were pink and she refused to meet Mick's gaze. Was she embarrassed, amused? Mick wanted to tilt her chin, see the emotion playing on her face and in her eyes.

"I understand. Perhaps we could do it later in the week?"

"I…"

Mick was sure she planned to refuse. Then her gaze dropped to Katie and she smiled, the expression filled with a sadness that tugged at Mick's heart and made him want to protect her from whatever it was that had hurt her.

"Sure, we can do it later in the week."

"Wonderful. Would Tuesday evening work for you?"

"Tuesday would be great. Can I bring something?"

"Jewelry stuff." Katie was nearly bouncing with excitement, and Mick put his hand on her head.

"Calm down, Katie. Portia might not have brought any of her jewelry supplies with her."

"Actually, I did. I'd be happy to bring them. Maybe we can make a bracelet together, Katie."

"I can't wait!"

"If six is good for you, Portia, Mick can give you the address while I get my rambunctious granddaughter into the car."

"Six is great. Thanks, Mrs. Campbell."

"We'll see you then. Come on, Katie, Jack, let's go. It's freezing out here."

Mick smiled and shook his head, grabbing a business card from his pocket and scribbling his parents' address on it. "Here you go. Call me if you decide you can't handle Mom and Katie's enthusiasm. I'll make your excuses."

He'd meant it as a joke, but she didn't crack a smile.

"You've got a nice family, Mick. I hope you know that." There was a wistfulness to Portia's voice that didn't match her bright shoes and wildly curly hair

"I do." Mick stepped closer, cupping Portia's face in his hands, so that she had no choice but to meet his eyes. Her skin was petal-soft beneath his palms, her eyes velvety dark. "What's made you so sad today? Not my family?"

"No, mine. But like I said, it would take a lifetime to explain it all." She stepped away from his touch, unlocked her car door. "I guess I'll see you Tuesday."

He wanted to say something to ease her tension and make her smile, but she pulled the door closed, waving as she drove away.

Maybe that was for the best. They lived different lives in different states. Probably had different values, different ideas about what family meant, what commitment meant.

But even as he told himself that, Mick knew he didn't believe it. Portia might have a life in New York, but her heart was with her family. He admired that about her. Admired her loyalty, her love for the members of the Blanchard clan. He only prayed that his investigation into Garrett McGraw's murder wouldn't destroy that.

NINE

Steel-gray clouds covered the sun as Portia drove back to the Manor. They matched her mood and the aching emptiness in her stomach. If she'd had a choice, she would have driven back into town, sat in the Beanery and sipped a steaming cup of coffee. But she'd already told two different families that she needed to be with Grandfather, so that's where she was going to be.

She sighed and rubbed the tension at the back of her neck. What had happened with Father had happened a hundred times before. She couldn't quite figure out why it had bothered her more today. Maybe it was being at church, seeing all the smiling, happy families and couples. Or maybe it was just that the older she got, the more she longed for something more: acceptance, belonging. A sense of home that she hadn't felt since her mother died—or disappeared, as it was turning out—when she was three.

But that was no excuse for acting pitifully, and that's how she'd felt when Mick and his family approached. What had Mick been thinking when he'd looked into her eyes? The moment had felt like so much more than it should have. Just remembering his warm hands against her cheeks and the intensity in his gaze made Portia's pulse race.

She'd wanted to stand there forever, looking into his eyes and letting him see the person she really was. And how foolish was that? In five days she was going back to her life in New York City. Add to that the fact that Mick wasn't her type, that he had a daughter, that he'd been married and had lost his wife and was probably still in mourning, and she had an entire truckload of reasons why she should avoid the man.

And she would. Come Tuesday, she'd call and make her excuses. The knowledge should have made her feel better. Instead, all she could do was picture Katie's disappointment. Okay. So maybe she'd make the decision about canceling later.

She shoved open the door to the Manor and walked inside and up to the third floor. Grandfather was sleeping, his gaunt, lined face nothing like what Portia remembered from her childhood. Then, Howard had been strong and quick, a man whose ruthless business dealings were well-known and even feared. Still, he'd loved his granddaughters and Portia had loved him. She still did. If only she could make things easier for him. She picked up his lax hand, stroked his gnarled fingers.

"I love you, Grandfather. And I'm praying for you."

Years ago, Howard would have scoffed at the words, insisting that prayers were desperate wishes whispered to a blind god. Now, even if he were awake, he wouldn't have responded, his pat answer lost somewhere in his failing mind.

Portia sighed and strode to the window. Outside, the

wind had picked up and light rain fell like tears from the blackening sky. If she hadn't been afraid she wouldn't be able to stop, Portia might have let a few of her own fall.

"What a crummy day."

"You're right about that." Miranda bustled into the room, her dark eyes red-rimmed with fatigue. "And it's going to get worse. The weatherman says sleet and snow for most of the evening and into tonight."

The weather hadn't been what Portia was referring to, but she went along with it anyway. "Yuck. I guess I'll be staying in for the duration. I hate driving in icy weather."

"Me, too. I offered to let the dayshift nurse go home, but she said she'd rather work doubles."

"I know, she told me when I came in. I sent her to the guest room for some rest while I sit with Grandfather."

"He doesn't look good, does he?" Miranda brushed thick white hair from Howard's forehead.

"No. He doesn't."

"I was hoping maybe it was my imagination that he's getting worse. I guess it wasn't."

"Last time I visited he looked pretty good. Now, I'm worried he might not be here at this time next year."

"He's lived a long life."

"I know," Portia ran a hand over her hair, "I just wish I could be certain about his eternity. It's so hard knowing his life is drawing to an end, but not knowing if he's ever made peace with God."

"It's something I think about every day, but Grandfather refuses to discuss it with me. I suppose I'll have to be content with that. There's lunch down in the kitchen. Why don't you go have something to eat? I'll stay with Grandfather for a while."

Portia wanted to refuse, but sorrow clogged her throat

and she simply nodded and fled from the room, afraid if she stayed any longer, the tears she'd held at bay would escape.

The house was silent as a tomb, the kitchen empty. Portia grabbed a bowl from the cupboard, served herself some of the ham and bean soup that simmered on the stove top and retreated to her room. She'd put off dialing the numbers she'd found on her father's phone bill. Now seemed as good a time as any to do so. The folded paper was tucked in her wallet and she pulled it out, smoothing the wrinkles, her fingers shaking at the reality of what she was doing.

Snooping. In her father's house. Looking for clues that would prove he'd been lying for the majority of Portia's life. And if she found proof of that, what other implications would it have? That he was a murderer?

No. Being a liar didn't prove that Ronald was capable of murder. It just proved that he wasn't the man Portia had believed him to be. Neither had Tad been, but that didn't make him capable of a horrible crime. She took a deep, shaky breath, trying to calm her rioting thoughts as she dialed the first number.

She wasn't sure if she should be relieved or disappointed when all three numbers turned out to be for skiing resorts. Obviously, Ronald had been planning his next vacation, not conducting underhanded dealings that might or might not have involved Portia's mother.

Which meant absolutely nothing. Despite coming up empty with the phone numbers, Portia was still convinced Ronald knew more about Trudy than he claimed.

"Portia?" Rissa knocked on the door and peeked into the room, her eyes shadowed, her skin pale. "You busy?"

"Nope. How was lunch?"

"The same as always. How's Grandfather?"

"Worse."

Rissa nodded and sat on the bed. "Listen, I want to tell you before I say anything to the rest of the family. I'm going home tomorrow. This place is just too dark for me. I need to get back to my life."

"I understand."

"Do you?" She sat down on the bed, playing with the soft folds of the duvet. "I hate to be a downer and ruin Winter Fest for you."

"You aren't." It had been ruined on day one when Mick had arrived with his questions about Garrett McGraw's murder. Things had only gone downhill from there. "I'll miss you, though."

"I'll miss you, too. The apartment will be quiet without you."

"And neat."

"That, too." Rissa smiled and stood. "I'm going to lie down. Lunch exhausted me. Father spent half of it berating Delia for not using her energy for the betterment of the company and the other half chastising Alannah for spilling the beans about Grandfather."

"So he knows? I'm glad I don't have to be the one to tell him."

"He knows. At least five people approached during lunch to ask about Grandfather's health. Father got the idea pretty quickly. How'd you know?"

"Mick told me."

"Mick, huh?"

"What?"

"You and the handsome detective seem to be spending an awful lot of time together."

"I saw him in Aunt Winnie's Sunday school class. If

you'd rolled out of bed at a decent hour, you would have seen him there, too."

"Your version of what a decent hour is is up for debate. And stop trying to change the subject."

"What subject? I saw Mick at Sunday school. That's all there was to it."

"And had coffee with him last night."

"And?"

"And nothing."

"Come on, Portia, there's more to it than that."

"No there's not, because Mick lives hundreds of miles away from SoHo *and* he has a daughter."

"No!" Rissa sat back down, her eyes wide and round. "Did you meet her?"

"She's six. Cute as a button and loves art and making jewelry."

"Mick's wife?"

"She passed away a few years ago."

"So, there's no problem."

"Of course there's a problem. I just got out of a relationship with a man who had a daughter."

"*And* an ex-wife. Big difference."

"Maybe, but I'm not in the market for a new boyfriend, so as a far as I'm concerned, Mick is just the detective who's investigating Garrett's murder." She hoped she sounded convincing, because she sure didn't feel it.

"Right. Tell me that again when I see you at the end of the week. Now, I really am going to lie down."

Portia closed the door after her sister, wishing she could be content to go back to New York to take up her life there, but as each day passed she felt less and less like returning.

Over the years, the noise and busyness of the city had

become as familiar to her as small-town life had once been. Still, there was a part of her that felt out of sync there, a part of her that longed for a slower pace, a quieter life. Perhaps that longing was God's way of telling her it was time to make some changes. Going to New York had seemed like such an adventure when she was young and eager to get out from under Ronald's control, but even then she'd known that Stoneley would always hold a special place in her heart. She just hadn't thought she'd ever return, hadn't imagined that one day she could live close to Blanchard Manor without feeling as if she was too much in her father's shadow.

Maybe it was time to reassess her life, but not tonight. Tonight, she'd spend some more time with Howard, maybe read for a while and hope that tomorrow would be better than today had been.

TEN

Someone was pounding on the door. The sound broke into Portia's sleep, pulling her from her dreams and waking her to darkness. She struggled out from under layers of blankets, her heart slamming in her chest. The lighted numbers on the alarm clock read just after three. Whatever was going on couldn't be good.

She hurried across the room, threw open the door. The hallway light was blazing. More light spilled from the third-floor landing. Portia blinked, trying to adjust her vision to the sudden brightness, her gaze focusing on the person who stood in front of her—Miranda, her face blanched, her eyes wide and dark. "Portia! Grandfather's missing."

"Missing?" The word made no sense. Howard barely left his bed, let alone his room.

"Yes. Gone. We've searched the entire third floor. He's not there."

"The rest of the house?"

"We're in the process of searching it." She raked a hand through her hair. "We need help, though. There are too many rooms. And if he's gone outside…."

"How could he have?" Portia shoved her feet into

boots, pulled a coat over her flannel pajamas. "He barely gets out of bed, and even if he did manage to get downstairs, we've got an alarm."

"Somehow he managed the steps. I don't know how far down he got, but when I checked the alarm, it was turned off."

"How long has he been gone?"

"I don't know. The night nurse says she went downstairs to get a cup of tea. She was gone maybe fifteen minutes. When she got back to Grandfather's suite, his bed was empty."

"Fifteen minutes isn't long. Is she sure that's all the time it took?"

"Who knows? She's hysterical. I can barely get a word out of her." Miranda spoke as she moved down the hall, knocked on Rissa's door. "We've got to find him. He's dressed in pajamas and slippers. No shoes. No socks. If he gets outside he'll freeze."

"What's going on?" Rissa stepped out into the hall, her silky nightgown covered with a robe.

"You explain, Miranda. I'm going to search downstairs." Portia raced down the stairs, worry a hard knot in her stomach. Outside, the storm had come full-force, rain and ice slashing against the windows as she searched one room after another and found each one empty. The front door was closed and locked. The back door the same. She couldn't imagine that Grandfather would have thought to bring a key and lock up after he left.

She unlocked the back door, shoved it open. Icy wind blasted into the kitchen, splattering the floor with water. She ignored the cold and the rain, flicking on the outside light and peering into the darkness beyond. Even the howl of the wind couldn't cover the sound of waves crashing against the cliffs. Portia could imagine how they would look—huge whitecaps slamming against rock. If Howard…

No, she wouldn't even think it. She was about to close the door, check the basement, when something just beyond the glow of the light caught her eye. White against the icy ground, it was too heavy to be moved by the wind. Portia squinted, tried to get a clearer look. Was it a piece of cloth? A plastic bag? Whatever it was, Portia couldn't shake the feeling that she should go out and examine it. She pulled her coat closer around her chest and raced out into the rain.

Mick came awake instantly, the shrill ring of the phone following him from his dreams into reality. He grabbed the phone, lifted the receiver to his ear, his gaze shooting to the alarm clock. Three-fifteen in the morning. Not a good time to be getting a phone call. "Campbell here."

"Mick? It's Drew." Drew Lancaster's voice was almost as surprising as the early-morning phone call. A fellow police detective, he often worked the same shift as Mick. His call could only mean that something big was happening.

"What's up?"

"We've got a problem at Blanchard Manor. Seems the old guy's gone missing."

"Howard Blanchard is missing?" Mick pushed aside heavy blankets and got out of bed, pacing across the room to stare out the window. Frozen rain and heavy wind made visibility almost nil.

"Yeah, his granddaughter says he's wandered off. They found his robe outside."

"You called the chief?" Mick grabbed clothes from the dresser, moving quickly, but silently. Kaitlyn slept soundly, but if she woke it would be difficult to get her back to sleep.

"Called him just before I called you. Roy's on his way."

"You're at the Manor?"

"Five minutes away. Things aren't looking good. Visibility is low. Temps around freezing. Depending on how long he's been out there…"

"So, let's hope he hasn't been out there long." Mick pulled a sweatshirt over his head, grabbed a rain parka from his closet. "I'll be there in twenty."

He made it in fifteen, thanks to his mother's willingness to baby-sit on short notice. She arrived six minutes after Mick's conversation with Drew and was in the kitchen making Kaitlyn's favorite banana muffins when he left two minutes later.

It was good to know his daughter was with someone who loved her. Not so good to know that eighty-six-year-old Howard Blanchard was wandering around in a winter storm. If the cold didn't kill him, the cliffs might. Finding the elderly man quickly was imperative.

Several SUVs were already parked in the Blanchard driveway as Mick pulled in. A few men dressed in black rain gear huddled on the porch. More were pulling gear from their vehicles. Mick grabbed his own gear and strode up the porch steps, nodding a greeting to Drew and Roy. "Any news?"

"Nothing good." Roy Marcell, the chief of police and Mick's boss, spoke above the howling wind and pounding surf. "Most of the family is already out searching. Winnie and Miranda were the only ones who had the good sense to wait for help."

"Which means we're searching for seven people instead of one." Portia among them. Mick refused to think about her wandering near the cliffs, the wind and freezing rain pelting at her. Icy wind, slick rocks and sleet would make the area treacherous, and Portia had an unfortunate propensity for losing her footing.

"We're searching for one. We've got to assume the rest of the Blanchards know the area and are dressed appropriately for the weather. Howard's out in pajamas and slippers. Let's concentrate our effort on finding him until we hear that someone else might be in danger." Roy made valid points, and Mick knew he was right. That wouldn't keep him from worrying about Portia.

"How far could an eighty-something, nearly bed-bound patient get? That's what I'd like to know." Drew glanced at his watch. "That, and how long has he been out there?"

"What's the family say?" Mick pulled a flashlight from his pack.

"Near as they can tell, he left his room thirty minutes ago. One of his granddaughters found his robe in the backyard at quarter past three." Drew shook his head. "We'll be fortunate to find him alive."

"The longer we stand here, the less likely that will be. Let's get this show on the road. I'll take Blake and Kasuoff and head across the road. Maybe we can find footprints in the muck." Roy glanced at Mick and Drew. "Which one of you wants to take the cliffs?"

"I will." Mick hitched his pack onto his back. "We have the hospital on standby?"

"Yeah. An ambulance, too."

"Good." Mick started down the steps, bracing himself against the frigid wind. "With so many people out in this mess, we may end up with more than one patient on our hands."

He didn't wait for Roy or Drew to respond, just started around the side of the house, praying he'd find some evidence that Howard had been there, some clue that would lead him to the elderly man.

"Grandfather!" Portia's teeth chattered on the word, but she refused to go back to the house. Below her, waves pounded against the rocks, the slickness beneath her feet making her heart lurch and skip within her chest. At her father's insistence, she hadn't begun her search near the cliffs, but footprints in the garden had led her this way. At least, she'd thought they were footprints. Now, she wondered if what she'd seen had been nothing more than impressions in the ice-crusted ground.

"Grandfather! Howard!"

She shouted again, but could barely hear her own voice over the wind and crashing waves. If her grandfather was out here, if he was conscious, he'd never hear her. The storm howled and screamed, slamming the trees, the earth and Portia. She shouted again and again, her voice growing hoarse, her heart thrumming a frantic rhythm. If they didn't find him soon they'd be too late.

They might already be too late.

"Please, God, let him be okay. Help us find him," she whispered the prayer, imagining her words carried on gusts of wind and soaring to the heavens. Sleet battered her face and melted in the strands of hair that had escaped from her hood. Icy rivulets ran down her neck, the chill seeping into her bones. She gritted her teeth to keep them from chattering and carried on, following the line of the cliffs, hoping that her cell phone would ring and one of her sisters would tell her that their grandfather had been found. But the phone didn't ring and she kept walking, moving farther away from the Manor. Where was Grandfather? Could he possibly have come this far?

It didn't seem likely and Portia had almost given up hope when the beam of her flashlight fell on something lying on the ground. She hurried forward, saw that it was a shoe and picked it up. No. Not a shoe, a slipper. "Grandfather!"

This time when she shouted, she thought she heard a faint reply. She turned, flashing her light across the ground, illuminating the area near the cliffs, then in the other direction, toward the trees that grew in dark clusters along the path that lined them. Adrenaline pumped through her, warming her blood and giving her the energy to continue. Her light shone on something huddled near the trees. Portia hurried toward it, her feet slipping and sliding on the thick layer of ice, hope and dread mixing together into terrible apprehension.

Trees bowed toward the ground as the true fury of the storm unleashed in a howling frenzy of wind and hail. Portia ran as fast as she dared, skidding the last few feet, her shoulder slamming into a tree as she struggled to stop her forward momentum. She barely felt the impact. Her gaze was on the mound of fabric at her feet. Dirty, sodden, shivering, Howard Blanchard barely moved as Portia wiped water and ice from his face. "Grandfather?"

He moaned, opened his eyes. "What are you doing here? Shouldn't you be at school?" He was shivering violently, his skin pasty in the beam of her flashlight, and Portia didn't know if his confusion was due to Alzheimer's or hypothermia.

"I have the day off. How about you? Shouldn't you be home?" Portia stripped off her coat as she spoke, dropping it around Howard's shoulders and pulling the hood up over his head. She had to get him home. Fast.

"Home? I'm meeting her at the cliffs just like I used to."

"Who?"

"Ethel, girl, who else would I be talking about?" He didn't resist as Portia helped him to his feet.

"Grandmother wouldn't be out here in the rain and cold. And it's dark. Why would she be here in the dark?"

Howard stared at her, his dark eyes flashing with stubborn determination. "She told me Ethel would be here, so she will."

"Who is she?" As she spoke, Portia eased Howard's arms into her coat sleeves, slid her mittens over his hands. Her boots were much too small for his feet, but she pulled them off so she could tug off both pairs of socks she'd put on before she'd raced out into the cold. "Lift your foot."

He obliged, leaning on her shoulder while she pulled the socks over his slipperless foot before replacing the slipper she'd picked up from the ground. She did the same with the other foot, pulling off his sodden slipper, putting layers of socks on before replacing it. It wasn't enough. Not nearly enough. "Come on, Grandfather, we've got to get you home."

"I can't go home. I told you, Ethel's going to meet me at the cliffs. We're going to dance in the moonlight just like old times."

"There isn't any moonlight tonight." She put her arm around his waist, urging him back toward the house. Even if he'd resisted, he wouldn't have had the strength to pull away. His waist was much too thin beneath her arm, his arm lying across her shoulder, bony beneath the thick down of the coat she'd given him.

Once he'd been larger than life, a strapping six feet tall with eyes that blazed from a harsh, intelligent face. Forcing him to do anything would have been impossible. Now, he simply followed, frail, weak and beset by illness and Alzheimer's.

She tightened her grip, sure she could feel him slipping away. He didn't seem to notice, just shuffled his feet through the slush, seemingly oblivious to the cold and the danger he was in.

She cleared her aching throat and spoke above the storm. "You always said Grandmother hated storms. Are you sure she planned to be out here tonight?"

Howard glanced around, as if suddenly noticing the weather. "You're right. Ethel never did like the rain. Said it made her blue." He wiped a mittened hand across his face. "She wouldn't be out here tonight, that's for sure. So why'd you tell me that she was?"

"I didn't." Portia clenched her teeth against the shivers that wracked her body. If she was this cold, Grandfather was in serious danger of frostbite and hypothermia. She wanted to hurry him along, rush back to the house, but there was no hurrying, just plodding, painful steps.

"If you didn't tell me that, then what are we doing out here?"

"Heading home."

"That's the first sensible thing you've said." His voice was raspy, his arm shaking violently. He needed a doctor. Probably a trip to the hospital. She had to get him out of the cold.

And they were moving much too slowly.

Portia dug into the pocket of the coat Howard now

wore and pulled out her cell phone, her fingers so numb with cold she could barely dial.

The phone rang once before it was answered, Miranda's breathless voice filling Portia's ear. "Hello?"

"It's Portia. I've found Grandfather."

"Thank goodness! Where are you? Is he okay? Do you need help?" The words poured out in a near shout.

"He's really cold, but conscious. I'm trying to get him home, but I don't know if we'll make it without help. We're moving too slowly and he's not dressed for the weather."

"Tell me where you are. I'll get someone to you."

"Maybe a mile north of the Manor. Near the cliffs. I think we're past Blanchard land, but it's hard to say. Everything looks different at night."

"A mile. Portia, that's not possible. Grandfather barely gets out of bed."

"It's not just possible, it's where we are. I don't know how he managed it, but he did. He said something about meeting Grandmother Ethel and dancing in the moonlight." With each step Howard leaned more of his weight on Portia. She struggled to keep them both upright as the wind whipped against their bodies.

"Ethel and the moonlight? He's in another era. Not here. Listen, there's a police officer here. He says to stay on course toward the house. There's a guy heading in your direction. He's got cold-weather gear and can help you with Grandfather until we can get a stretcher out to you."

"Call an ambulance. Grandfather is going to need to go to the hospital."

"I will. I'll call his doctor, too. I think it'll be best if he's there when Howard is admitted."

"And Peg. Grandfather will feel better if she's at the hospital when he gets there."

"All right. Are you going to be okay? It's a mess out there."

"I'll be fine. Just get some hot chocolate ready. I'm cold to the bone." Which wouldn't have been the case if she'd taken the time to change before she plunged out into the storm. Instead, she'd just thrown a sweatshirt over her flannel pajamas, pulled on double layers of socks, grabbed her hat and mittens and left. She'd counted on finding Howard close to the house, assuming he wouldn't be able to get far.

A potentially deadly mistake.

She'd lived in Maine for enough years to know how to dress for weather like this, but panic had made her forget everything but her concern for her grandfather. Unfortunately, what was done couldn't be undone. She'd just have to muddle through until help arrived. All she had to do was keep moving toward the Manor, keep Grandfather on his feet and they'd both be fine.

In theory, it was a great plan. Unfortunately, Grandfather was a leaden weight, pulling Portia down with every step, and Portia knew that if help didn't arrive soon, she wouldn't be able to keep going.

ELEVEN

Five minutes later, her legs nearly collapsed from under her as Grandfather sagged against her side. His eyes were closed, his breathing labored. Where was the guy who was supposedly heading their way? Had they missed each other?

She trudged forward a few more steps, almost carrying her grandfather. "Come on, Grandfather. We can do this."

Howard moaned, but didn't open his eyes, and Portia's concern grew. She pulled the phone out again, knowing that help would arrive when it arrived, but needing to feel that she wasn't alone. Her fingers were stiff with cold, her hand uncooperative and the phone slipped from her grasp, falling to the ground and sliding outside the beam of the flashlight. Her heart skittered in her chest, panic gnawing at her stomach. What if she couldn't make contact with someone? What if Miranda had misunderstood her and sent the search party south? What if—

"Stop it!" She hissed the words, searching the ground with the flashlight, the beam jerking and jumping as her arm trembled. There it was! She took a step forward, stopping short when a shadow shifted just beyond the light. She squinted, not sure she'd seen anything, hoping that perhaps rescue was at hand. "Hello?"

Nothing moved. No one answered. She played the light along the ground, then along the line of trees. Something flashed white in the shadows, then disappeared from view. A face? Portia blinked, trying to clear her vision. "Is someone there?"

Her muscles strained to keep Howard upright, her legs trembled with fatigue, but she moved one shuffling step after another, backing away from the trees and whatever they concealed. There. She saw it again. A flash of movement that could have been nothing, but that made her heart jerk in her chest and her body tense with fear. She eased to the side, keeping her gaze and the flashlight on the trees. If she had to run, she wanted to be prepared, though how far she'd get with her grandfather, a dead weight on her arm, she didn't know.

Someone caught her arm, pulling her up short and Portia screamed, swinging the flashlight hard, catching a glimpse of a tall, dark form as a hand closed over hers and the light was pulled from her grip.

"Hey, it's the cavalry. I thought you'd be happy to see me."

Mick.

If Portia hadn't been holding on to Howard with every bit of strength she had left, she would have thrown herself into his arms. "Thank goodness! I thought help would never get here."

"I made tracks as soon as I heard where you were. We've got a team coming in with a stretcher for your grandfather. We'll wait here for them." His voice was soothing and calm, his leather-clad fingers still wrapped around hers. "How's he doing?"

"Not good." Her voice caught on the words.

"Let's take a look." Mick's flashlight illuminated Howard's grizzled face, his half-closed eyes, the too-short coat Portia had wrapped him in. "Hold him for another couple of seconds. I've got thermal blankets in my pack. We'll do our best to warm him up."

And warm Portia up, too. Mick tried not to let his worry show as he pulled the blankets from his pack. Specially designed for cold-weather rescues, they offered a barrier to both the moisture and the cold. Mick laid one on the ground, then helped Portia ease Howard onto it. He used another blanket to cover the elderly man from chin to feet. "You next."

He didn't give Portia time to argue, just tugged her over, opened the blanket and gestured her down next to her grandfather. "Lie down next to him. You two can share body heat."

"Body heat? I don't think I've got any." She was shivering so hard her teeth knocked together as she spoke.

Mick pulled off the hat he wore and knelt down beside her. "Let's see if we can keep any more of it from escaping." He ran his hands over her soaked, ice-coated hair, brushing off as much water as he could before easing the hat onto her head. Then he pulled out the umbrella he'd shoved into his pack and opened it, shielding Portia and her grandfather from the sleet.

Howard's eyes were closed, his skin pasty in the light from Mick's flashlight. He didn't look good. Portia didn't look any better, though her eyes were open, staring into Mick's. "Do you think he'll be okay?"

"I don't know."

"He's been failing for a while. This could be too much for his system to take."

"We'll get him back to the Manor, then to the hospital." He wanted to give her reassurances, promise that the grandfather she loved, that she'd come out in a storm to save, would be fine, but Howard was eighty-six, in poor health and fragile. Whether he could survive this assault to his system, Mick couldn't say.

"He wanted to dance in the moonlight with my grandmother. That's why he was out here." Portia sniffed and Mick was surprised to see her eyes filling with tears. She always seemed so tough, so sure of herself.

He pulled off a glove, brushed heavy wet curls from her cheek. "Dancing in the moonlight. That must have been a nice dream he was having."

She nodded, tried to smile, her lips tinged blue from cold. "He said they used to do it all the time."

"They must have been quite a couple."

"From what I've heard, they were." Her eyes drifted closed, then opened wide again. "Too many late nights. I can barely keep my eyes open."

"Try to for a little longer." His palm lay against her cheek, absorbing the frigid temperature of her skin.

"I will. I have to. At least until Grandfather is safe."

"He will be in no time. I see lights. It looks like his transportation is almost here."

"Finally." She pushed aside the blanket, making sure not to let any cold air get to her grandfather as she scooted out on her knees. She was still shivering, the sweatshirt she wore drenched and hanging almost to her knees, the worry and fear in her eyes obvious. "I need to call Miranda. Make sure his doctor is waiting at the hospital. Where's my flashlight? I dropped my phone and—"

"And if we don't find it before we go back to the house, we can come back tomorrow and look."

"But—"

"You've done everything you could. You found him, you got him the help he needed." He held the flashlight under his chin, unbuttoned his coat with one hand, shrugged it off and draped it around her shoulders. "Button up."

"You'll freeze."

"I've got enough layers to keep me warm until we get back." Which wasn't really true, but there was no way he was going to wear a coat while Portia was cold.

She didn't seem to hear his response, her gaze was on the trees that she'd been backing away from when he'd found her. "Did you see that?"

"See what?" He was still crouched over Howard, blocking the older man's face from the sleet with the umbrella, but he swung the flashlight toward the area Portia gestured to. The trees were dark with shadows, pine boughs heavy with ice dipping toward the ground and obscuring Mick's view of whatever it was she'd seen.

"I don't know. I thought something moved."

"The way the wind is blowing through the trees, everything is moving."

"I guess so." She didn't sound convinced and her gaze remained on the trees.

Mick kept the light trained in the same direction, moving it as far up the treeline as it would go. Deep shadows and thick pine branches were a perfect cover for anyone who might choose to hide there. But who would? And why?

"No one" was the easy answer. Even as Mick watched, the shadows of the trees danced and swayed, ice and snow crashing from their branches. Portia was nearing hypothermia, had been out here alone with her grandfather. It was possible fear was playing tricks on her mind. Possible. "Tell me exactly what you saw."

"Just shadows moving." She hesitated.

"But…?"

"But right before you got here I thought I saw a face staring out from the trees." She shook her head. "It was my imagination. I'm sure of it."

"Where'd you see it?"

"Almost straight across from where we are, but it was nothing much, just a glimmer of white in the beam of my flashlight. It could have been anything."

She thought it was something. Mick could see it in the tense way she held her shoulders, the way her gaze returned to the trees, then darted away again. In the distance, lights bobbed and bounced as the rescue team approached. Once they arrived and Portia and Howard were on their way back to the Manor, Mick would check the area for signs that someone had been lurking in the woods. For now, he'd play things down, make sure Portia didn't have anything more to worry about than her grandfather's health. "Visibility is low. It's possible you caught a glimpse of a deer."

"Sure." She placed a hand on each of Howard's cheeks, leaning close to him as if she could will her heat into his body. "He's so cold. When is the rescue team going to get here?"

"They're almost here. Look." He gestured to the lights that were drawing closer.

"Finally." She stood as the crew approached, stepping back to let the paramedics load Howard onto the stretcher. Her already thin face looked gaunt; her hair was a sodden mass plastered to her neck and cheeks. She looked frail, her body dwarfed by his coat, and

Mick put an arm around her shoulders, feeling fragile bones and tight muscles.

"He'll be okay."

"I hope you're right." She shivered beneath his arm, her teeth chattering.

"Go on with him. You need to get warm, too."

"What about you?"

"I'm going to find your phone."

"I thought you said we'd find it tomorrow."

"It *is* tomorrow."

"You'll freeze."

"I will if we keep standing here discussing it, but if you hurry up and get going, I can start the search and we'll both be inside and warm in the next few minutes."

"Since you put it that way." She smiled and hurried after the rescue crew.

Mick pulled a poncho from his pack, tugged it on over his flannel shirt, searched the ground until he found the cell phone and headed into the trees. Even with the light, the blackness was darker there, the air redolent with pine. The ground, frozen and covered in a layer of ice, would show little in the way of footprints, but Mick didn't let that stop him from searching. He moved a few feet in and a few feet up, the flashlight illuminating the ground in front of him, his eyes scanning the frozen pine needles and slushy muck.

As he'd expected, there was little to see, though one deep indentation made him pause and bend close. Feet or knees could have created it, though he saw no tread marks, no visible footprints. He scanned the area surrounding the spot, looking for more evidence that a person had stood or knelt there, but if someone had, there was nothing more to indicate it.

He should be relieved, glad to put the idea to rest, but

as he stepped out of the trees into the open, he couldn't shake the feeling that he'd missed something, that Portia had been right, and someone had been watching from the shadows.

A harsh crack sounded from somewhere behind him, and Mick whirled, adrenaline racing through his veins. More than likely a branch had given under the weight of ice and wind, but maybe not. One way or another, he was going to find out. But he wasn't going to be a moving target while he did it. He flicked off his flashlight and started back toward the trees.

TWELVE

"Mick?" Portia's voice carried over the sound of rustling trees and the ping and splatter of sleet hitting the ground. He froze, waiting for her to call again, hoping she wouldn't, hoping she'd turn around and go back the way she'd come. He'd figured Portia was safely back at the Manor by now, wrapped in warm blankets and drinking coffee. Or, and he'd thought this more likely, hurriedly dressing so that she could ride to the hospital to be with her grandfather. The fact that she was here was an unexpected complication and he needed to think through what he was going to do about it.

"Mick?" She was coming closer, probably following his tracks in the ice and slush. Knowing her tenacity, she'd keep following them until she found him and whomever it was Mick was hoping to find. He wasn't sure why he was so certain that someone else was near. There was no telltale movement, no way to hear breathing or rustling cloth over the sound of the storm. Yet someone waited, of that he was sure. His nerves hummed with awareness, his muscles fluid and ready to move. Only the thought that Portia was coming up behind him kept him still.

Should he keep heading forward or go back? In other circumstances he wouldn't have hesitated, would have stalked his prey until he caught him, but these weren't normal circumstances and he couldn't risk leading Portia into danger.

He stepped back from the shifting shadows, his gaze never leaving the blackness and eased away from whatever had been waiting for him.

"Mick!" Portia shouted as loudly as she could, though her throat felt raw and sore. There were footprints in the icy slush and she followed them to the edge of the woods, fear shivering up her spine as she stared into the blackness beyond the beam of her flashlight.

Where *was* he? Not back at the Manor. She would have seen his light if he'd passed her as she'd come back outside. "Mick!"

The storm raged, tossing her voice toward the cliffs and the crashing pounding ocean waves. She should be thankful the prints she was following didn't lead in that direction. The ground here was slippery enough. Any closer to the edge of the cliff would be downright dangerous. Not that following the footsteps into the woods seemed any safer.

Strange. She'd spent fifteen years of her life at Blanchard Manor, had run along the cliffs, explored the woods, often been out after dark and in the rain, yet she couldn't recall ever feeling the kind of fear she felt as she peered into the shadows that weaved and swayed beyond her light. Her hand trembled, bouncing the light from one tree to the next, one dark crevice to another. Each time she was sure she'd see something—a face, a person. A monster?

Was Mick in there? And if he was, why wasn't he answering? Should she go after him, or go back to the Manor and find help?

The questions raced through her mind as she took one cautious step after another into the depth of the trees. "Mick?"

Something moved in the blackness just beyond the reach of her light. A strange shifting of shadows that was nothing and yet so real she was sure it was coming toward her. She took a step back, stumbling over a root or fallen branch, desperately trying to catch her balance, the beam of her light sliding along the ground, up toward the sky, to her left. Illuminating pine needles, tree trunks. A face.

She screamed, racing back the way she'd come, her feet flying as fast as the icy ground would allow, any sounds of pursuit muffled by the storm's fury.

Something snagged the back of her coat, jerking her backward with enough force to pull her off her feet. She would have fallen, but strong arms wrapped around her waist, tugging her back against a solid chest. Mick. She knew it before he spoke, could sense it in the gentle way his hands held her waist, the calm, even rise and fall of his chest.

She sagged with relief, allowing him to support her for just a moment before she straightened and turned to face him. "You scared me half to death."

"Sorry about that."

"I forgive you. This time. Next time I might give you more than a high-pitched squeal."

"Squeal? If that's a squeal, I'd hate to hear you scream." He smiled and snagged the flashlight from her still-shaking hand. "Are you all right?"

"Fine."

"Good. Want to tell me why you're out here instead of at the Manor warming up, or at the hospital with your grandfather?"

No, because then she'd have to admit that once she'd learned she wouldn't be able to travel in the ambulance with her grandfather, she'd begun to worry about Mick. "I thought you might need your coat back."

That was the truth. She just wouldn't expand on it.

"So you came to give it to me. And here I thought you were worried about me being out here on my own."

"You're a cop, Mick. I knew you could take care of yourself."

"Thanks for the vote of confidence. And you're right, I *can* take care of myself, but a night like this isn't a good time for anyone to be outside. Come on, let's get back to the Manor before we both freeze. Here," He used his teeth to tug his glove off, then tucked the flashlight under his arm. "Your hands are ice-cold. Let's get my gloves on you."

He eased the glove onto her hand, his movements practiced and efficient, as if he'd done the same a thousand times before. And he probably had. Portia could imagine him helping Katie in the same way, but she wasn't Katie and the gesture seemed much too intimate for her peace of mind.

She pulled her hand from his grasp, did her best to get the glove onto her cold, clumsy fingers. "Thanks. I can manage."

"Let's get out of here, then. I'm sure you're anxious to see how Howard is doing."

"What about my cell phone?"

"I already got it." He pulled the phone from his pocket and handed it to Portia, then trained the flashlight on the ground, grabbed her hand and tugged her forward, walking quickly and forcing her to do the same.

"Did the rest of your family get back to the Manor all right?" There was something in Mick's voice that made Portia wish the light was shining on his face and she could see his expression.

"Yes, they were all waiting when Grandfather and I arrived. Why?"

"Just wanted to make sure we didn't need to go searching for anyone else."

She didn't think that was the only reason for the question, but she was too cold and tired to push for more. "Everyone is fine. How about Katie? Is she with your mom?"

"Yeah, that's one of the blessings of living so close to family and having parents so willing to give of their time."

"Even at three in the morning?"

"Even then." He smiled down at her, dropping his arm around her shoulder, the gesture so comfortable, so right, Portia didn't have the strength to pull away.

"Tell me how your grandfather managed to get out of the house." He spoke easily, barely winded by the brisk walk and the driving sleet.

Portia's own lungs were on fire, the cold searing them more with each breath. "I don't know the whole story. From what I've gathered, his nurse went to the kitchen to get some tea and he disappeared."

"Has he wandered before?"

"Not that I'm aware of, but it's not uncommon for Alzheimer's patients."

The lights of the Manor shone up ahead, beckoning through the darkness, warm, inviting. All the things the Manor had never been. Portia wanted to run toward it anyway, but her feet were clumsy logs, barely carrying her forward. She stumbled, and Mick pulled her closer to his side.

"Are you going to make it, or do you need a lift?" His breath was warm against her cheek.

"A lift? You don't seriously think you could carry me all the way back." She tried to laugh, but her throat was raw and it sounded more like a cough.

"I think I can do whatever it takes to get you back home."

Home? Stoneley had never been that, either, but Portia couldn't define the reasons for it, let alone explain them to someone else. "Fortunately, you won't have to. I'll make it just fine."

One step at a time, one breath at a time, she'd manage. And maybe that was the best way to handle finding answers to the questions about her mother and about Garrett's murder. One slow, careful step at a time. Eventually, she'd uncover the truth. She just hoped the truth didn't destroy her family.

THIRTEEN

A hot shower hadn't eased the chill that had invaded Portia's bones. Despite layers of clothing and two cups of coffee, she was still freezing, her hands aching with cold, her feet numb. Aunt Winnie had wanted her to stay at the Manor, smothered under heavy quilts and sipping hot soup, but Portia couldn't bear the thought of being warm and comfortable while Grandfather was being poked and prodded at the hospital. The fifteen-mile ride to Stoneley Memorial Hospital took just under forty minutes, the sleet and wind making driving difficult. Now that she was in Grandfather's room, there was no way she planned to return to the Manor before he woke, no matter how many times her sisters and father told her she'd be better off there.

And they *had* told her that. Over and over again.

"We're going to get some coffee, Dear. Come with us." Aunt Winnie placed a hand on Portia's arm, concern aging her as time had not.

"I can't drink another cup." And she didn't want Grandfather to wake up in a strange room alone.

"Maybe not, but you *need* another cup. You're still shivering."

"Can you bring me one back, then? I don't have the energy to move."

Winnie studied her for a moment, her hazel eyes seeming to see much more than Portia wanted to reveal. Finally, she nodded. "Of course. And how about something to eat?"

Portia wanted to say no, but knew her aunt would persist until she agreed. "Anything is fine."

"All right. We won't be long. Come on, my girls."

My girls. They'd always been that to Aunt Winnie. Not her nieces, or her brother's children, but her girls. Winnie had put her time and her passion into raising Portia and her sisters, giving selflessly and never expecting anything in return. It was from her that Portia had learned what true love meant, but all Winnie's love couldn't dispel the unhappiness and discontent that seemed to haunt the Manor.

And it was that which had driven all but Miranda away. Portia sighed, staring out the hospital-room window. Gray and bleak, the morning held no promise, the sky steely and cold, sleet slashing down onto the pavement and cars below. The scene matched her mood perfectly, the harsh rawness of it mirroring the way she felt each time she visited Blanchard Manor. Yet, unlike Rissa, Portia couldn't seem to make a clean break, couldn't quite give up on her childish dream to make a life for herself in Stoneley.

"Get me out of this bed and get me on my feet." Howard's voice was raspy and weak, breaking into Portia's thoughts and causing her pulse to leap with relief. If Grandfather was awake, he couldn't be that bad off. Could he?

"You're awake. I was starting to worry."

"About what?" He struggled to rise, his feeble efforts barely lifting him from the pillows.

"You. Now lie back. You've had a hard night and the doctor said you need to rest."

"Rest? Rest? Your father is trying to get rid of me. My own son, trying to kill me. How can I rest?"

"Father would never hurt you." Portia was shocked at the accusation, though she'd been warned that Howard could sometimes be paranoid.

Howard didn't seem to hear her defense of Ronald as he struggled to sit up and slide his legs over the side of the bed. "I need to get to the office. Make sure all the papers are in order."

"Everything *is* in order, Grandfather. You've already taken care of everything."

He stared at her for a moment, his eyes blank. "Did I?"

"Yes. You did. That's why you really need to rest, now." She squeezed his hand.

"Maybe I do. I *am* tired." He subsided back onto the bed, all of his energy drained. Perhaps the same thing had happened when he'd left the house—a burst of energy and strength that had carried him down the stairs and a mile from home, only to desert him.

"Who are you, anyway? I don't know you, do I?"

The question cut like a knife, the knowledge that Howard didn't know who she was filling Portia with sadness. "I'm Portia, your granddaughter."

"Can't be. If my little Portia was all grown up I'd be an old man." His eyes closed, his breathing evening out and as quickly as that he was asleep again.

She stayed where she was, her hand wrapped around his, remembering when things had been different, when she'd been the one who needed comforting and Grandfather had been the one to offer it. His days had been filled with work and responsibility, but at night, when Portia worried about monsters in the closet and beneath the bed, he'd searched every corner of her room for her, never downplaying her fear or belittling her for it.

A tear escaped and trickled down her cheek. She wiped it away, tried to hold back even more. Grandfather would hate to see her cry. Especially, if he was the reason for her tears.

A quiet knock sounded against the already-open door and Portia turned, expecting to see a nurse. Instead, she saw Mick, prickly stubble on his chin, fatigue accenting the hollows beneath his cheeks. He scanned the room, his gaze resting on Howard before meeting Portia's.

"How is he doing?"

"Okay." She lowered her eyes, hoping any evidence of her tears was gone. "The doctor said he's in surprisingly good shape considering what he's been through."

"I'm glad to hear it." Mick pulled a metal chair across the room and sat down next to her. "How about you?"

"I'm cold." And tired and discouraged.

"Here, maybe this will help." He took off his leather bomber jacket and put it around her shoulders. It smelled liked him—clean, outdoorsy, masculine—the warmth of it seeping through her sweater and easing her chill. "Is that better?"

"Yes, thanks."

"Good, now maybe you'll tell me why you're crying."

"I'm not."

"You were." He ran a finger down her cheek. "Are you worried about Howard?"

"Yes." And so many other things. "It isn't easy watching someone I love disappear."

"Is that what it feels like to you?" His fingers stroked the sensitive skin behind her ear, his palm warm against the tense muscles of her neck and the ice that had invaded her bones melted.

"Exactly like that. It's as if everything that Grandfather is has faded away and soon there'll be nothing left but an empty shell."

"Not empty. Your grandfather will always be in there, Portia, even when he's hard to find."

"Will he? It doesn't seem that way. Not when he looks at me and doesn't know who I am."

"Maybe his mind loses you for a moment, but in his heart, he'll always know who you are."

"You sound like you know."

"My wife's father had Alzheimer's. Even at his worst he was comforted by her presence. Unfortunately, after her death, his health deteriorated rapidly."

"I'm sorry."

"So was I. I stayed in Portland until he passed away. Then came home to be with my folks. Death has a way of making us appreciate life more, of making us appreciate those we love more, too." His hand dropped to her arm, rubbing the length of her bicep as if trying to warm her.

She thought about telling him there was no need, that he'd already managed to warm her as nothing else had, but decided that was information better kept to herself. "I think I appreciate Aunt Winnie's presence in my life all the more because my mother…"

She'd almost said "died," but couldn't complete the thought.

"Your aunt is a great lady. She's always the first to volunteer for church and community functions. There aren't enough people like her in the world." He stood, pacing across the floor, his sudden tension telling Portia something was coming. Something she might not like.

"Listen, I hate to bring this up after everything that happened last night, but it's going to come out eventually and I want you to be prepared."

"What?"

"I've found some interesting information about Blanchard Fabrics. If Garrett discovered it, we might have found a motive for his murder."

All the warmth she'd been feeling fled and Portia stood. "What are you talking about?"

Before he could speak, hushed voices and padding feet sounded from the corridor and Aunt Winnie, Delia, Rissa and Juliet returned. Their timing couldn't have been worse.

"Mick, I didn't know you were going to be here. I would have brought some coffee for you." Aunt Winnie seemed oblivious to the tension in the room, her face creased in a smile, her hazel eyes shining with pleasure. Knowing her propensity for matchmaking, she was probably hoping Mick's presence might mean good news in the romance department for Portia.

"It's okay. I've already had my limit this morning." Mick smiled, relaxed and apparently undisturbed by the interruption.

"Then maybe you'd like to have a donut or a Danish? I brought plenty. Stay and have one." She set a white box on the bedside table. "After all, you did to help bring Father home safely, I feel like we should offer you something."

"Getting Howard home safely was a joint effort. No one involved has any need to be repaid."

"Be that as it may, Ronald and I will be looking for an appropriate way to say thank you. Here's your coffee,

Portia." She handed Portia the foam cup. "You look pale, dear, I really think you should go home."

"I'm fine." Except that her pulse was racing, her mind scrambling for an explanation for what Mick had said. What could he possibly have found that might be worth killing over?

He walked toward the door, smiling, relaxed, looking for all the world as if he hadn't just pulled the rug out from under Portia's feet.

"I've got a desk piled high with paperwork I need to get back to, so I'd better take off." Mick took a step toward Portia as he spoke, leaning in close to her ear as he pulled his jacket from her shoulders. "We'll talk later."

Portia waited twenty endless minutes, chatting with her aunt and sisters, doing her best to act carefree and relaxed. Rissa wasn't buying the act. Portia could see it in her twin's eyes. She wanted to ask what was going on, but didn't want to do it in front of the others. Instead, she shot Portia a few curious glances, but remained silent. Which was just as well. Portia had no intention of saying anything until she'd spoken to Mick.

Finally, she couldn't wait any longer. She stood, stretched. "I'm really not feeling myself. I think I might take off for a while."

"Are you ill?" Winnie pressed her hand against Portia's forehead, feeling for a fever the same way she had when Portia was a child. "You're not warm, but you do sound a little hoarse."

"I think I'm just exhausted."

"Go on back to the Manor and get some rest, then. And drive carefully. It's wicked out there today."

"I'll be careful." She dropped a kiss on Winnie's head, waved goodbye to her sisters and hurried out of the room.

FOURTEEN

Mick stepped into his office and was tackled from behind by a pint-sized tornado.

"Whoa!" He staggered back, turned to scoop his giggling daughter into his arms. "That's it, Katie-bug. It's out into the cold with you."

"No! Daddy! No!" She squirmed and laughed as he shoved open the office window. "Put me down. Grandmom will be mad if I get my dress all messed up. She ironed it and everything."

"Did she?" He slid Kaitlyn down onto the floor and surveyed the dress she wore. "And she did a good job of it, too." Not like his own rushed and harried attempts usually were. "Where *is* Grandmom?"

"Right behind you. So if you've got something negative to say about me, you'd better wait a while." There was laughter in his mother's voice and Mick turned to pull her into a bear hug.

"Thanks for taking care of Katie for me this morning. I know 4:00 a.m. is a bad time to get yanked out of bed."

"Three-thirty. Not that I noticed the time or anything." She smiled, her eyes the same blue as Katie's, the dimple in her cheek only making the resemblance between grandmother and grandchild all the more noticeable. "And you know your father and I are happy to help out. It's nice to have Katie around. She's an easy little girl to entertain."

"Most of the time." Mick watched his daughter twirl around the room, her fingers skimming over papers and desk, chair and window. The chubby baby she'd been at three was gone, replaced by a sturdy little girl. She was growing up fast and he wasn't quite sure how he felt about it.

"She's easy all the time. How is Howard doing?"

"Barring any unforeseen complications, he should make a full recovery."

"I'm glad to hear it.

"Me, too. He didn't look good last night. I was worried things might not go well for him." Mick shrugged off his coat and settled into the chair behind his desk, snagging the back of his daughter's coat and pulling her into his lap. "So, what brings you here? I thought we agreed no more visits before school."

"This was important, Daddy."

"Important, huh?"

"You forgot to sign my permission slip. Mrs. Samuels said if I don't bring it back today I can't go on the field trip."

"Mrs. Samuels also said that if you didn't stop talking out of turn, you'd be in detention on field-trip day."

"I've been working really hard at being quiet." Katie's eyes were wide and so innocent it almost hurt to look into them.

"Then I guess I'll sign the slip."

"Thanks, Daddy!" She threw her arms around him, squeezing hard. He hugged back, inhaling baby shampoo and banana muffins. He wanted to freeze-frame the moment, the sweet earnestness in her face when she put her hands on his cheeks and looked into his eyes, the high-pitched timbre of her voice when she spoke. "You be careful today, okay?"

"Aren't I always?" He chucked her on the chin. "*You* be good for Mrs. Samuels."

"I will be. I promise."

"Good. Now go on with Grandmom and have a good day. I love you."

"Love you, too, Daddy."

"Am I interrupting?" Portia peered in the open doorway, her hair a wild mass of curls, her pink wool coat unbuttoned and splattered with rain.

"Not at all. We were just leaving, weren't we, Katie?" Debbie smiled at Portia and reached for Kaitlyn's hand.

"Yes, I've got school today."

"School is fun, right?" Portia squatted down until she was eye to eye with Katie.

"I like art best, but we don't have that on Monday."

"But you've got plenty of other things, kiddo, so you'd better get moving or you'll be late." Mick put his hand on her shoulder, moving her toward the door.

"You're going to be at Grandmom's house tomorrow, right?" Katie kept speaking as Mick urged her into the hall.

Portia hesitated and Mick was sure she wanted to say no. "Yes, I am."

"And we're going to make bracelets. I've got turquoise and silver beads Grandmom bought me."

"I love turquoise."

"Do you have beads you can—"

"Katie, you're going to be late. Go on with Grandmom."

She heaved a sigh but obeyed, waving goodbye as she disappeared down the corridor.

"She's awfully cute." Portia's gaze was on Katie's retreating figure and Mick was sure he saw sadness in her eyes.

"And awfully precocious."

"You say that as if it's a bad thing."

"Only sometimes." He gestured to the coffeepot sitting on his desk. "Coffee?"

"I think I've had my quota for the year. Poor Aunt Winnie thinks coffee, tea and soup will cure whatever ails a person."

"It might not cure a person's ills, but it sure can go a long way in waking someone up. Especially this stuff." He poured a cup, took a sip. "Want to have a seat?"

"You haven't asked me why I'm here."

"Did you think I'd need to?" Mick's half smile made Portia's heart jump and she made a production of sitting in the chair across the desk from him, arranging her coat around her legs, placing her purse on the floor. Anything but meet his all-too-knowing eyes.

"You're uncomfortable. Why?"

"No one wants to hear bad news."

"I don't think that's the reason." He covered her hand with his, stopping the tapping of her fingers against the desk. "Is there something about me that bothers you? Other than the fact that I'm investigating Garrett McGraw's murder, I mean."

Everything. His rough-hewn good looks, his love for his daughter, the obvious respect he had for his mother and for everyone else who crossed his path. They were all an elaborate trap that she was terribly afraid she was about to walk into. "Of course not."

He studied her, his palm warm against her knuckles, his expression unreadable. Finally, he leaned back in the chair, his hand slipping from hers as he reached for his coffee cup again. "I'm not sure I believe you, but I'm not going to push you for the truth. You're here to find out what I've learned about Blanchard Fabrics. I guess we'll just stick to that."

She wanted to tell him the truth, tell him that she was afraid of what she felt when she looked into his eyes. Instead, she straightened her spine, ran her hand over the wild, sodden curls that refused to be tamed. "What *did* you learn?"

"Nothing so bad in the grand scheme of things, but in light of McGraw's murder, the information may be important." He grabbed a file folder and held it out to her. "The information is in there. Blanchard Fabrics wasn't originally owned by your grandfather. It began as a company called Celtic Seasons."

"That's not possible."

"I'm afraid it is. Celtic Seasons was a start-up, doing well for a while, but suddenly losing revenue. By the time Howard bought it, the owner had two choices—sell or go bankrupt."

"I've never heard of Celtic Seasons." The deep cold she'd felt for most of the day crept up her spine and shivered into her soul. Her entire life, Portia had been hearing stories about how Grandfather had taken a risk, started a company and built it up by pure Blanchard grit and determination. Legend. Lore. Truth. She'd thought it all those things. Was it possible that Grandfather had lied? That, like her father, Howard had secrets he'd lied to keep hidden?

"I doubt many people have. The original owner was

a man named Lester Connolly. The documentation is all in the folder."

Portia opened it, stared at the pages, but could make no sense of what she was seeing. "Can I have this?"

"Sure. I made that copy for you."

"Thanks. I'd better go. Grandfather might wake up again and I should be there." She tried to keep her expression neutral, tried not to let him know how quickly her heart was beating, or how her stomach twisted and churned.

He knew, though. She could see it in the sympathy that shone from his eyes. But she didn't want or need his sympathy. All she wanted was the truth.

"It might mean nothing, you know." He spoke quietly, his words meant to soothe, but doing nothing to still the frantic rhythm of her pulse.

"It means my grandfather lied. That all these years when he was talking about hard work and determination and going after your dreams, he hadn't done any of those things."

"He might not have founded the company, but he worked hard to build it into what it is. Nothing can change that."

"He still *lied*. To me. To my sisters. To my father and aunt. To customers. To everyone." She shoved back from the desk, started toward the door, not knowing where she was headed, but knowing she needed to get out.

"Portia." Mick grabbed her arm, pulling her to a stop before she could leave. "Your grandfather might have lied, but he's still the same man. A man you obviously love."

"Yeah, I do love him." She swiped at tears and tugged her arm away. "But that doesn't change what he did. It's funny, every man I've ever loved has turned out to be a liar. Or maybe it's not funny. It's just sad. I've got to go. Thanks for the information."

She ran out into the hall before he could respond, ran down slick steps to the sidewalk, ran to the Bug and climbed inside, but she couldn't run from what Mick had told her. The folder he'd given to her sat on the passenger seat, a coiled snake ready to strike a fatal blow. Portia wanted to throw it in the nearest trash can and forget she knew anything about it. But she couldn't. Too much was at stake.

Portia pulled back into the parking garage at Stoneley Memorial Hospital, moving by rote, not knowing what she'd say when she saw her sisters, not knowing if she'd say anything at all. Maybe the best thing she could do was wait until she had calmed down and had some time to think things through.

She rested her head on the steering wheel, closing her eyes and trying to pray. The words wouldn't come, her thoughts refusing to coalesce. Whatever God wanted her to do in this situation, whatever He expected from her was unclear. Finally, she pushed open the car door and headed back into the hospital.

Aunt Winnie was the only one still there. She looked up as Portia arrived, her hazel eyes bloodshot from lack of sleep. "You came back. I was hoping you'd gone home."

"I wanted to visit with Grandfather again before I did."

At her words, Howard shifted in bed, his dark eyes open. "It's about time. I thought you weren't coming."

"I was here earlier. Remember, Grandfather?"

"Of course, I don't remember. My brain's gone."

Portia smiled at that. "Not so far gone that you can't give me a hard time."

"The day that I can't is the day they bury me. Get me some water, will you, doll?"

"Sure. You look like you're feeling better."

"Better? I'll be better when they let me out of this place." He sipped the water, eyeing Portia and Winnie. "You go on home, Winnie. Portia will stay with me."

"I don't mind staying, Father."

"Well, *I* mind you hovering over me like a mother hen. If you don't want to go home, go get yourself something to eat. You look wrung out."

The words were harsh, but the affection in Howard's gaze was obvious. He might not be exactly the man Portia had believed him to be, but he did love his children and grandchildren.

"I *am* tired." Winnie glanced at the clock on the wall. "Peg will be here in half an hour. Portia, if you can stay until she gets here, maybe I'll go nap and return later."

"I'll stay. You go rest." Portia kissed her aunt on the cheek, waited until she walked out of the room and then settled on a chair near her grandfather.

"You look beat, too, doll. I guess my little stunt exhausted everyone but me." Howard's eyes were black onyx, dark and brilliant.

"You're exhausted, too, Grandfather. Even if you refuse to admit it and rest." She lifted his hand, held it gently, the fragile bones and parchment skin showing his age the way his eyes didn't.

"I'm on borrowed time. I don't want to waste too much of it sleeping."

"You've got plenty of time, Grandfather."

"Only someone as young as you would say so. We older people call it like we see it, and the way I see it is that I'm nearing the end of a very long road."

"But a good one, right?" Portia's throat was tight with tears, but she refused to cry.

"A decent one. I've got children and grandchildren to carry on with what I started."

It was the perfect segue and Portia couldn't ignore it. Not when she knew her grandfather's lucidity wouldn't last and that if she hesitated there might never be another opportunity.

"You really built something great with Blanchard Fabrics." Her voice shook with nerves, but she didn't think he noticed.

"I did. Wasn't easy, either."

"Were there other people in our family who were in the industry? Into fabrics, I mean."

"Not that I know of. Seems to me I'm the first, but not the last. Your father's doing an all-right job at keeping the business running."

"He is. Grandfather…" How could she possibly say it? How could she tell him that she knew he'd lied?

"Spit it out, doll."

"Have you ever heard of Celtic Seasons?"

For a moment he said nothing, just watched her, his gaze unwavering. "Yes. But not many other people have. Where'd you hear the name?"

"A…friend."

"And what else did this *friend* tell you?"

"That a man named Lester Connolly started the company, was building it up and doing quite well. Then somehow almost went bankrupt."

"It happens to small businesses all the time."

"And people buy those businesses all the time, but most of them don't lie about what they've done."

Howard's face paled. "No. I suppose they don't."

"Then why did *you*, Grandfather? Why not just tell the truth? That you bought a failing company and made it into a successful business. That's no less of an accomplishment."

"Because there was more to it than that." He sagged back into the mattress, his face suddenly slack, his eyes vague.

"Grandfather? Are you okay?"

He blinked, his gaze clearing once again. "I'd hoped you'd never find out. I'm not proud of it. Not at all."

"What are you talking about?" Portia wanted to run from the room, leave Howard and his secrets for someone else to deal with. Only the thought of Mick's words, of his implication that those secrets might have led to the private investigator's death, kept her in place.

"Connolly and I were best friends when we were kids. We grew up together, went to school together, played ball together. We even double-dated. If things had been different we might have gone into business together."

"What happened?"

"Gladys happened. Funny, I can't even remember what it was about her I found so attractive. All I know is that back then, she was the woman I planned to marry. Lester, he felt the same. We argued, even had a fistfight about it, but in the end it wasn't up to him or me. Gladys chose and Lester was the one she wanted."

"But you met Ethel, fell in love with her, got married. I thought *she* was the love of your life."

"Oh, she was. My Ethel was the best thing that ever happened to me, but by the time I met her it was too late."

"Too late? What are you talking about, Grandfather?"

"I was angry. Hurt. Bitter. And I had the means to take the only thing besides Gladys that Lester valued."

"Grandfather, what did you do?" Portia felt ill, her stomach churning with the sick, sure feeling that there was much more to the story than even Mick knew.

"I'd inherited money from my father. I used it to hire some people to do what I didn't have the guts for. Go into the factory, sabotage some of the machinery. Nothing obvious. Just little things that held up production. A few too many unhappy customers and Lester couldn't pay his bills. He had a choice, sell cheap or go bankrupt. I made him an offer he couldn't refuse."

"You forced him out of business?" What could she say? What did she want to say?

"Do you hate me for it, doll?" He stared into her eyes, his gaze deep and hiding more secrets than she ever could have imagined.

"Of course I don't. How could I? You're my grandfather."

"And a liar. A cheat."

"What happened was a long time ago."

"A long time ago. Yes, it was. Sometimes I've even been able to believe the stories I told all of you about the company and have almost forgotten the way Blanchard Fabrics came about. Sometimes." He closed his eyes, opened them again. "I know you're disappointed. I don't blame you for it, but I hope you'll forgive me."

"You didn't commit a crime against me, Grandfather."

"I lied to you."

"But it's the Connollys you really hurt."

"Don't you think I know that? Don't you think I've thought of a million ways to make it up to them, to say I'm sorry? But it's too late. It was too late the minute I conceived the idea." His voice rose, his grayish skin flushing with anger as he raised up on his elbows.

"It's okay, Grandfather."

"No. No, it isn't." He subsided, his eyes closing.

"What's going on in here? Don't you know it isn't good for your grandfather to get so worked up?"

Portia spun around to face Peg as the nurse hurried into the room.

"Are you okay, Mr. Blanchard?" She shot Portia a sharp look and reached for Howard's wrist, checking his pulse.

"I'm fine. Stop fussing." But Howard didn't open his eyes and his voice was soft, almost slurred.

"What you need, Mr. Blanchard, is a nice cup of tea and a few hours of rest. I brought you some of your favorite blend from home. Let's see if I can find some hot water." Peg hurried out of the room and was back a few minutes later with a cup. "Here we go. Now, let's get some nice tea into you and then you can nap."

"Nap? Do I look like a child?" Howard opened his eyes, the flashing irritation in them obvious.

"Peg is right, Grandfather. A few hours of rest will do you good." Portia kissed her grandfather's forehead and smoothed his hair.

"It would do you good, too, Portia. Why don't you go home? I'm sure your grandfather will be able to rest more easily if the room is quiet." It wasn't a subtle dismissal and on any other day, Portia might have chosen to ignore it, but she had to talk to Winnie and her sisters, see what they thought of Grandfather's story. Portia knew what *she* thought. If Garrett McGraw had found the same information as Mick, if he'd threatened to go public with it, Ronald could have done whatever was necessary to protect Blanchard Fabrics. Even if that meant murder.

Portia hurried out of the room, her throat tight, her

eyes burning with tears. It was hard to know that her grandfather had lied and harder still to know that he'd sought revenge by destroying a man's business. But worst of all was the nagging doubts about her father. Believing that he'd lied about her mother's death was bad enough. Now she couldn't help wondering if he was also capable of murder.

FIFTEEN

"Lester Connolly? Are you sure you didn't misunderstand, dear?" Aunt Winnie sat on the loveseat in the parlor, her foot tapping against the floor, her face leached of color. For the first time in Portia's memory, her aunt looked older than her years. Knowing that it was her retelling of Howard's story that had stolen the color and life from her aunt was a hard, persistent ache in her chest.

"I'm afraid not. It's all here in the paperwork Mick gave me." Portia passed the papers to her aunt, watching her face as she flipped through the documents. The room was unnaturally silent, her sisters sprawled on sofas and chairs, all looking as shell-shocked as Portia felt.

"The name is here, but perhaps these documents are phony." There was little hope in Winnie's voice and less in Portia's heart.

No matter what her sisters or Winnie might choose to believe, she knew the truth. "Grandfather verified what's in those documents and more."

"So, Grandfather's been lying to us all these years. I guess I should be surprised, but I'm not. After all, Father must have gotten his ability to fabricate stories from someone."

"Delia!" Winnie's voice was sharp, her eyes flashing with anger. "Your father didn't *fabricate* anything."

"I'm afraid none of us agree with that, Aunt Winnie." Juliet put an arm around her aunt's shoulders. "Our mother is alive somewhere and we just can't believe that Ronald didn't know."

Bianca rubbed the back of her neck and paced across the room. "This doesn't look good, you know."

"To whom?" Miranda sat in the recliner, stiff and tense, her hands fisted in her lap. "Who would even care but us?"

"Anyone and everyone who has an interest in Blanchard Fabrics. Think about it—we've run entire ad campaigns based on our company's honest, straightforward approach to business. When it gets out that the supposed founder of the company is a fraud, Blanchard Fabrics is going to suffer." Bianca strode toward the door, her lawyer-persona firmly in place. "I've got to call Leo. Tell him what's happened." Even in the midst of the crisis her face softened as she mentioned Leo Santiago. The two had connected at Aunt Winnie's sixtieth birthday party—after years of casual acquaintance—and had been inseparable ever since.

"You're not going to tell him what Grandfather did to Celtic Seasons, are you? How can you be sure he won't tell every tabloid from here to Boston?" Delia followed Bianca to the door, her words hushed but insistent.

"Because I know. But, if it will make you feel better, I'll only tell him what's in the legal documentation." She ran a hand over her thick strands of brown hair and sighed. "If Garrett McGraw found out that Grandfather sabotaged a company to get where he is, he might have thought the information was a gold mine. And if he approached Father, who knows what Father's reaction might have been…" Her voice trailed off and she hurried from the room, her words hanging heavy in the sudden silence.

"No, I won't believe Ronald is capable of such a thing." Winnie was the first to speak. Then, as if a dam had burst, the rest joined in.

Portia didn't add to the frenzy of heated whispers. There was nothing she could say that would change things, nothing that could convince anyone that Winnie was right. Everything they thought they knew about their family was based on a lie. In light of that, almost anything seemed possible.

"I'm going to the cliffs." Portia raced out into the hall and away from all the things she couldn't change.

The sleet and rain had stopped, replaced by cold, gray mist that clung to the ground and hung in the trees as Portia made her way to the cliffs. She hadn't bothered bringing her paint or easel. She knew she would find no solace in them. What she wanted was simple— to be alone, to think without the cacophony of voices that seemed always to be part of her relationship with her sisters.

Bundled up against the cold, a scarf protecting her face, she barely felt the sting of arctic air as she spread a plastic tarp on the ground and lowered herself onto it. Gulls screamed and swooped, calling to one another in a harsh and haunting symphony, their white bodies stark against the charcoal sky. Far below, waves crashed against the shore, the timeless rhythm of the place, the untouched beauty of it, stirring Portia's soul.

"Your aunt said I'd find you here. She thought you might be painting." Mick's voice carried over the sound of the gulls and waves moments before he settled down on the tarp beside Portia. "It's a beautiful place for it."

She nodded, afraid if she tried to speak, tears would choke her. She wasn't surprised that he'd come, and couldn't be upset by his presence. Being alone had seemed the right thing when she'd left the house. Now, it felt good to be with someone else.

To be with Mick.

It was a truth she wasn't sure she was ready to accept. Risking her heart so soon after having it broken wasn't something she was prepared to do.

"A beautiful place to paint, but you didn't bring a brush or an easel, or even a sketchpad." His hand slipped under her scarf, cupping the nape of her neck, the cold leather of his glove making her shiver.

She had the urge to lean in close to him, inhale his warmth and strength. Only recent disappointments kept her from doing just that.

He didn't speak again, just sat beside her, his hand on her neck forging a connection that words could not. The silence between them stretched out, comfortable and so familiar Portia felt as though she'd been here forever, sitting with this man, sharing nothing and everything all at once.

It was more, so much more, than any single moment out of the millions she'd spent with Tad. How that could be, Portia didn't know. She rested her head on up-drawn knees, closing her eyes and listening to the gulls, the ocean, the slow, easy pulse of her heart. She needed to go back to the Manor, face her sisters and aunt again, try to find a solution to their problems, but sitting here with Mick was so much easier.

"Eventually, you'll have go back." His voice was gentle, his hand stroking down the length of her hair.

"I know, but not yet."

He cupped her cheek with his hand, urging her to face him, his eyes so filled with compassion Portia had to look away.

"I'm sorry my investigation has caused so much pain for your family."

"Your investigation didn't cause anything. My father and grandfather managed to do it all by themselves." She sniffed, wiped away unwanted tears and stared out past the cliff's edge, far out to the horizon where gray sky met gray-blue ocean, the colors blended, yet separate. "I've always thought families should be like the horizon—completely different elements touching each other and meshing into one cohesive picture. Mine has never been like that. We're more like the gulls calling to each other as we pass by. Always searching, but never quite finding what we want."

"What do you want?"

"Me?" She met his eyes, smiling past tears that continued to fall. "I want the horizon, the dreamy beauty of it, the complexity and the simplicity. I want to know where God wants me and I want to be there. Not rushing around trying to figure it out." She stood, knowing Mick was right, that she had to return to the Manor and all its darkness and chaos. "But I'm sure listening to me go on about my life is *not* the reason why you're here."

"Are you?" He folded the tarp, tucked it under his arm, the wind ruffling his hair, his harsh features stark and un-yielding. "Because it's exactly the reason I'm here."

"Mick—"

"Would it be such a bad thing to think that I came here to make sure you were okay?"

"Yes, because if I start thinking about it too much I'll build it into something it's not."

"You'll build it into exactly what it is: me and you creating a bond that we might not have asked for, but that's there anyway." He put a hand on her arm, stopping her when she would have walked away. "There's something between us, Portia. Why pretend it isn't there?"

"Because my heart has already been broken once this year and once was plenty." She tried to smile, tried to pretend the conversation was like any other, not filled with emotions she'd rather keep hidden.

"If someone broke your heart, he was a fool. I don't plan to follow in his footsteps." He leaned forward, his hand cupping her face, his lips brushing hers, the warmth of them washing through Portia and filling her with the sense that this was where she was meant to be—standing on the cliffs, the wind tugging at her hair, the man she loved holding her close.

Loved?

Impossible. She barely knew the man and he barely knew her.

Portia pulled away, almost stumbling in her haste. "I've got to get back. Aunt Winnie's probably worried and I'd hate for her to come out in this weather to find me."

"She knows you're with me." But Mick walked with Portia anyway, wondering who had broken her heart, wondering even more what had possessed him to kiss her. Knowing she lived in New York should have been like seeing a flashing neon sign every time he looked at her: Off Limits.

Unfortunately, even a neon sign plastered to her forehead might not have been enough to keep him away. A few days ago, Mick's only interest in the Blanchards was in trying to figure out how they might be connected to McGraw's death. He hadn't planned on it being any more than that. But there was one thing he'd learned over and over again in life. God didn't always give what was planned or expected.

Sometimes He gave even more.

Mick glanced at Portia, saw her cheeks flushed with pink, her eyes still shimmering with tears. She looked small and fragile beneath the heavy yellow parka she wore. The scarf she'd thrown around her neck was a hodgepodge of colors and textures, all bright and cheerful against the backdrop of the gray day. Even the bright colors couldn't hide her mood or the quiet melancholy that clung to her.

Whatever Mick's thoughts, whatever his feelings, the best thing he could offer Portia right now was time to accept the changes that were happening in her family and space to figure out what those changes would mean for her.

While she did that, he'd do everything he could to find the person responsible for McGraw's murder. Unfortunately, Portia's father was one of his prime suspects. "Did you tell your family about Celtic Seasons?"

"I told Aunt Winnie and my sisters. I'm not sure any of us want to tell Father."

"There's no need. I'll be visiting him at the factory later today."

"I doubt he'll be happy to see you there. Bad press and all that." She sounded tired, and Mick wrapped his arm around her shoulder, felt the delicate bones beneath her coat.

"Is that what it's all about to him? Protecting the company name?"

"What you're really asking is if I think he'd commit murder to keep the company from getting more bad press."

"Do you?"

"I wish I could say no, but the truth is, I don't know. My father is…my father. He plays by his own rules. I don't think those rules include murder, but I just don't know."

"Don't give up hope that he's innocent. I'm still investigating other leads." Most of them hadn't panned out, but there were still a few that deserved checking. Mainly ex-cons who McGraw had arrested and who had either served their time or were out on parole.

"Other clients of his?"

"No." He hesitated. "But McGraw had his share of enemies. On the surface, he was a nice guy, but not everyone liked what was underneath."

"You sound like you knew him well."

"We grew up together." And that was as much as he would say. McGraw's widow deserved to live her life without the stigma of his failures hanging over her head.

They were at the Manor and Mick used that as an excuse to forestall the conversation. Talking about McGraw always filled him with both guilt and anger. Once, McGraw had been full of promise. How he'd gone on to waste what he'd been given was something Mick didn't even pretend to understand. "I've got to head back to my pile of paperwork. I'll call you if anything comes up. You do the same for me."

"All right. Thanks for keeping me updated and for…" She shrugged, shivered and wrapped her arms around her waist. "Just thanks."

"You're welcome. Now go inside before you start

shivering more than you already are and I have to lend you my coat again."

She laughed, the sound throaty and full, much larger than he would have expected from a woman her size. It reminded him of the night he'd first seen her laughing on the ice, her colorful, mirror-trimmed skirt shimmering in the fading sunlight. Had it only been three days ago? It seemed he'd known her longer, that everything about her was a mystery and, yet, something he intuitively knew.

He wanted to kiss her again, capture the laughter on her lips, taste her joy. He bent, brushed his lips against hers and this time she didn't pull away. Instead, her arms wrapped around his waist and she burrowed closer, stealing his breath and any hope he had of walking away from her with his heart intact.

Finally, he eased back, looked down into her flushed face. "I'll see you tomorrow."

"Tomorrow?"

"My parents' house for dinner. Katie's expecting to make bracelets with you."

"Of course. See you then."

Portia turned and fled into the Manor, the feel of Mick's lips still warm on hers. His scent, the scratchy feel of his beard, all thrumming through her blood as she closed the door. Whatever happened in the next few days, Portia was sure of one thing—she was going back to New York on Friday and she was going to forget all about Mick, because if she didn't, she was afraid her heart just might get broken again. And this time would be a lot worse than the first.

SIXTEEN

Mick had gone to bed too late. He was willing to admit it. A brief discussion with Ronald Blanchard had yielded little more than what he already knew. He'd spent hours on the computer researching Celtic Seasons and Blanchard Fabrics and tracking the felons McGraw had arrested. Several were out on parole. Two hadn't checked in with their parole officers last month. Whether or not that was important to his case, Mick didn't know. By the time he'd finished, the sky was silvery purple and streaked with gold and he was frustrated. A few hours of sleep hadn't eased the feeling, and now, six minutes before Katie's school bus arrived, he was pouring cereal into her bowl with one hand, shaving with the other and reminding himself that it wasn't his dawdling daughter's fault that he was running late.

"Hurry and eat, Katie. We're running late." He tried for patience as he prodded her for what seemed like the fiftieth time.

"I'm not late. I'm dressed already. Look." She stuck her foot out from under the table. "I've even got my shoes tied."

"Good job. Now eat."

"But Daddy, I don't like this kind of cereal."

"It's what we have."

"But—"

"Kaitlyn Rose, eat your cereal or we won't be going to Grandmom's for dinner tonight. If we don't go to Grandmom's, you don't get to make bracelets with Portia."

She shot him a baleful look, but spooned up some cereal. "Grandmom said oatmeal is healthier than this stuff. She made me some with brown sugar yesterday."

"That's because Grandmom wasn't running late." He put a glass of orange juice in front of her. "Four minutes."

To her credit, she finished the cereal, brushed her teeth and was ready to walk out the door three minutes later.

"Got your backpack?"

"Yep." She held up the bag.

"Lunch?"

"In my bag."

"Homework?"

"Yes."

"Brain?"

"You always ask me that." She smiled, showing the dimple in her cheek.

"Just want to make sure you don't leave anything behind."

"I've got everything."

"Good girl. And just in time, too. Here comes the bus."

Mick walked her outside, kissed her on the cheek and watched her board the bus. She was growing up. There was no doubt about that. Problem was, Mick wasn't ready for it. He'd enjoyed the sweet baby years, the challenges of toddlerhood, the excitement of preschool years, but now he was in unknown territory, dealing with a girl who would one day become a woman.

"And what I know about women could fit into a thimble." He mumbled the words as he walked around the side of the house. The sight that met his eyes froze any further words in his throat. Someone had slashed the tires on his SUV and shattered the windshield.

His heart slammed in his chest, rage clawing at his gut, but years of experience schooled him to do the job that needed to be done. He strode to the SUV, peered in the side window and saw a paper-wrapped brick inside. It took seconds to open the door, seconds longer to pull on gloves and grab the note. Its message was written in blood-red ink:

Stop investigating McGraw's murder or someone you love will be next.

The threat was obvious.

He called the school first, asked the principal and teacher to meet his daughter's bus and escort her into the school. Then he called Drew and the state crime lab technicians. If there was forensic evidence to be had, they'd find it.

And then they'd find the person who'd left it behind.

Mick could only hope that person wasn't part of Portia's family. Unfortunately, the fact that the threat had come a day after Mick had approached Ronald at Blanchard Fabrics seemed like too much of a coincidence not to follow up on.

Portia found the Campbells' house easily and parked at the curb. A Queen Anne with blue vinyl siding and a white wraparound porch, it looked homey and inviting. Still, she sat in the car for a few moments, gathering her nerve and lecturing herself on the best way to conduct herself around Mick. Ignoring him seemed childish, but spending too much time talking to him was asking for trouble. And kissing him again was completely off limits, number one on her list of things not to do. Not that she expected there to be an opportunity. With Mr. and Mrs. Campbell and Katie around, Portia and Mick wouldn't have any time alone.

And that was exactly the way she wanted it.

The front door of the house opened before she got out of the car and Mick stepped onto the porch. He wore jeans and a long-sleeved flannel shirt, his hair spiking up. Despite his height, he walked with an easy grace, moving across the yard in a few long steps and peered into the window.

She cracked the window open. "Hi."

"Hi yourself. Are you planning to come inside or stay out here for a while longer?"

"I'm coming. I just had to get my stuff together." She rolled the window back up, grabbed the bag of beads and tools and pushed the door open.

"Need some help with that?"

"I've got it. Want to take these for me?" She held out the bouquet she'd brought for his mother.

"For me?" He took the flowers, his mouth quirking, his gaze touching her hair, her sage coat, her charcoal slacks before returning to her eyes. "And I thought you didn't care."

"I don't. They're for your mother."

He laughed and offered his hand, his palm warm, the rough calluses on it rasping against Portia's skin as he pulled her from the car. "My mother will love them. Listen," He stopped on the porch. "I need to talk to you before we go in."

His eyes were the deep, stormy blue of the ocean, and Portia knew that whatever he had to say wasn't going to be good. "Has something happened?"

"Someone left me a message this morning. The note said I should leave off the McGraw murder case or someone in my family will be next."

"Katie." Portia's stomach knotted, the thought of Mick's little girl being the target of a killer terrifying her as nothing else in the past few days had.

"That seemed to be the implication. The fact that this happened the day after I discovered your grandfather's lie seems like an odd coincidence." He leaned against the porch rail, his voice grim, the overhead light casting his face into shadows.

Did he suspect her? Or someone in her family? "What are you getting at, Mick? Do you think *I* had something to do with it? Because I didn't. I'd never make a threat like that. Not against anyone, but especially not against a child." Her heart thudded painfully, her stomach twisting and turning, but she refused to look away.

"It never even occurred to me that *you* would." Mick grabbed her hand, pulled her into a tight embrace. She could hear his heart beating beneath her ear, feel the quick rise and fall of his chest. "But there's someone else in your family that crossed my mind."

"My father."

"Who else?"

"I don't know, but I can't believe my father would stoop to threatening a child. It has to have been someone else."

"Was he home last night?

Was he? He hadn't been when Portia went up to bed and he'd been gone when she went down for breakfast. "I don't know."

"It's something I need to know. I'll stop by in the morning—"

"No, I'll ask Aunt Winnie when I go home. She'll know. Then I'll call you."

"Portia, it's my job. I can't have a civilian asking questions that are part of my investigation. Let me do it my way. I promise I won't make things any more difficult for your family than they have to be."

"I—"

"There's a murderer on the loose. Whether that person is someone in your family or not, he's getting desperate. I don't want you to put yourself in the middle of things. It's too dangerous."

"I already am in the middle. I've been in the middle of it since you came to our house to question the family." The front door opened before she could say any more and Katie peeked out.

"You're here!"

"I am." Portia smiled at the little girl, her pulse racing as she thought of what had happened to Garrett and what *could* happen to the precious child standing in front of her. "And so are you. I like your skirt. Pink is a good color for you."

"It's my favorite. I brought my beads. Did you bring yours? Grandmom set up a special table for us and everything, but if you didn't bring anything, that's okay. We can just enjoy having you for a visit."

Someone had coached the girl, but couldn't teach her to hide what was in her eyes. If only adults were as easy to read. "I did bring some things I think you'll like working with."

"Great, because I told all the girls in my class that I was making a bracelet with a real artist, so—"

"Here, Katie." Mick handed the flowers to his daughter. "Take these to your grandmother, please."

"Oh, they're beautiful. She's going to love them." Katie skipped back into the house and Portia turned back to Mick.

"What happens now?"

"With the investigation? I keep doing what I've been doing and pray that eventually I'll find the guy I'm looking for."

"But Katie—"

"I've got a friend who's a retired cop. I already put a call in to him. He's driving up from Maryland and should be here sometime tomorrow night. He'll watch out for her when I can't be around."

"I still don't like it."

"Neither do I, but it is what it is." He shrugged. "Part of being a cop. If I quit cases because of threats, I wouldn't be very good at what I do. Come on. If we don't get inside soon, my mother will send my father out instead of Katie."

"Your mother sent her?"

"My mother is almost as excited by your visit as my daughter is." He steered her toward the door.

"Is she into jewelry, too?"

"No, she's into me. My life. Matching me up with someone. She's invited at least five women over here since I moved back to town. I've always found a way to get out of it—paperwork, Katie had too much home-work, I had to pull an extra shift."

"So what happened tonight? Did you run out of excuses?"

"No, I didn't want to make one." With that intriguing comment, he pushed open the door and led her into the house.

SEVENTEEN

After dinner, Mick stood in the doorway to the parlor watching Portia and his daughter, their heads bent close together, their attention focused on the beads spread out in front of them. They were completely in tune, each one as passionate about the stones as the other. They'd already made Katie's charm bracelet, though if Mick's daughter had her way, they'd do another. And another and another.

"Daddy, what do you think?" Katie held up two beads. "Do you like the blue or the pink? The pink is quartz."

"You know I'm not much for jewelry, Katie, but that pink does match your skirt." And Portia's cheeks, but Mick didn't think she'd appreciate him saying so.

"That's what I was thinking." His daughter beamed with pleasure, her toes tapping with excitement as she pulled another quartz bead from table and put it in the pile of beads Portia had said she could keep. It was a pile that was getting bigger by the second.

"Don't be greedy, Katie. Portia was nice to bring so many things for you to look at, but that doesn't mean you get to keep them all."

"She's fine." Portia met Mick's eye and he was surprised by the sadness in her gaze. "But I'm really exhausted. I hope none of you mind if I head out."

"Of course not, Dear." Mick's mother stood. "I'll just get your coat."

Mick's father stood, too, stretching and running a hand over his salt-and-pepper hair. "Thanks for coming, Portia. It's been a pleasure getting to know you."

"Thank you, Mr. Campbell, I feel the same." Her smile was genuine, but she hurried to gather her things, leaving the beads out on the table. "Katie, I think you should keep all of those. I've got plenty at home."

"Really? Can I, Daddy?"

"You can."

"Thank you, Portia! You're the best." She threw her arms around Portia and Mick was sure Portia stiffened. Odd. He'd been sure she'd connected with his daughter. Now it seemed as if she couldn't wait to get away.

He followed her out to her car, took the keys from her trembling hands and opened the door for her, blocking the opening when she moved to get in.

"Is your hurry to leave something to do with that broken heart you said you're suffering from?"

"I'm tired. It's been a long day."

"Portia, you know I'm not going to believe that. Why not just tell me the truth?"

"Because the truth makes me look like the biggest fool alive."

"I doubt that." He traced the frown line between her brows, the curve of her cheek. "We all make mistakes. What was yours named?"

She lifted a raven brow and smiled. "Tad."

"Tad."

"And Jasmine. His daughter. And then there was Anna, the ex-wife."

"He had a daughter and an ex?"

"You don't have to say anything. Everyone in my family told me what a big mistake I was making, but I wouldn't listen. He just seemed to fit my life so well."

"But?"

"But he wanted a babysitter more than he wanted a girlfriend. Jasmine needed a mother figure and I was willing to step in and help out."

"He knew you'd grown up without a mother."

"He played that card well and often."

"Until you got wise to him?"

"Until his ex decided she was done 'finding herself' and wanted to come home. She was living with them for three weeks before I found out."

"I'm sorry."

"Not as sorry as I am. I wasted two years of my life in that relationship, probably spent more time with Jasmine in those years than her father did. Now, they're a happy family and I'm," she sighed, the sound shaky and broken, "I'm here."

"With a broken heart?"

"Only sometimes. I really need to go, Mick."

"I won't keep you." He slid his hand away. "But I want you to know something."

"What's that?" She slid into the car.

"My interest in you has absolutely nothing to do with your ability to entertain my daughter." He shut her door before she could respond and watched as she drove away, hoping she hadn't sensed the anger and disgust her story had invoked in him. Portia had said she'd been a fool. Mick thought she had it backwards. Tad was the fool. And his loss might just be Mick's gain.

Mick's words rang through Portia's head as she drove home. He'd seemed so sincere, the anger burning in his eyes telling her exactly what he thought about Tad and his actions.

But hadn't Tad always seemed sincere? Hadn't he often seemed angry on her behalf, taking her side and supporting her through tough critics and frustrating customers?

Of course he had. But in the end, his loyalty was only a show, his feeling that his daughter needed a mother far outweighing his affection for Portia, or any true desire he had to support her.

She sighed and raked a hand through her hair. She had too much on her mind. Thinking about Mick would have to wait. Tonight was a charity dinner that all the Blanchards except Miranda and Portia were attending. If she were going to look at Father's day planner to see where he'd been yesterday, now was the time to do it. And while she was at it, she might as well search for information about Trudy. Friday would be here soon and she wanted answers before she returned to New York.

If you return.

The thought whispered through her mind, refusing to be dislodged. Several months ago, she'd been offered a fair price for her arts and craft store. She'd refused to sell, but now wondered if she should. The money she'd receive from the sale would be enough to make a fresh start somewhere else. A new beginning. It sounded good. So good she could almost imagine herself doing just that. The problem was, her imagination was filled with Stoneley, with the rugged shoreline and treacherous cliffs, the harsh winters and brightly colored falls, with the renewal of spring and balmy summer breezes, with the slow, easy pace of small-town life.

And with Mick.

"Stop it. You are not moving back to Stoneley to be near a man. If you want to try something new, find another place to do it," she muttered the words as she stepped into the Manor. Her feet echoed on the marble floor. Aside from that, the silence was complete—no voices, no footsteps, no dishes clanging in the kitchen. Now was the perfect time to look for the information about where her father had been when Mick's car was vandalized.

She found nothing in Ronald's office. No daily planner, no scribbled notes, no files with Trudy's or Garrett's name, nothing that would implicate Ronald and nothing that would exonerate him. Which meant she'd have to check the office at Blanchard Fabrics. She grabbed a spare key from her father's desk, tucked it into her purse and walked out of the office. Tomorrow night she was working a booth at the Winter Fest. After she finished, she would stop by Blanchard Fabrics and see if she could find anything. While she was there she'd look for information about her mother.

If she felt a little guilty, she refused to admit it to herself. For almost twenty-three years she'd thought her mother dead. Now it seemed Trudy was alive. If it took digging through her father's things to find the truth about what had happened so many years ago, Portia would do it.

Still, she was nervous as she pulled into the church parking lot the following night. Thinking about searching through her father's work office was one thing. Actually doing it was another.

"Portia!" Aunt Winnie hurried toward her, a smile creasing her face. "There you are. Doris Wilson's got you working the ring-toss booth. Do you need help finding it?"

"No. I'll manage. Thank you, though. You're doing the bake sale?"

"Isn't it what I do every year?" She smiled again, but there was a sadness in her eyes that Portia had noticed often in the past few days.

She put her arm on her aunt's shoulder. "Are you okay, Aunt Winnie? You seem down lately."

"I'm fine. There's just so much going on it's hard to concentrate on anything else. Finding out your mother might not have died in that accident, learning that private detective was murdered, then Father escaping the house. It's a lot for an old lady like me to assimilate." She didn't mention the revelation about Blanchard Fabric's beginnings and Portia took her cue and kept silent about it, too.

"You're not old, Aunt Winnie."

"I'm sixty." She shook her head. "It's so hard to believe. I'm past that first blush of youth, past childbearing and child-rearing. So, what's left for me? This." She waved a hand at the festivities. "Always being the maiden aunt, working the bake sales and fundraisers and watching others have what I can't."

"Aunt Winnie—" Appalled, Portia reached for her aunt, but Winnie stepped back, laughing lightly.

"There you go. Me being maudlin. It *must* be winter, so many dark, dreary days." She patted Portia's cheek, looking her carefree, happy self once again.

"Are you sure that's all it is, Aunt Winnie?"

"Of course, dear. I…" Her voice trailed off, her gaze fixed on a point beyond Portia's shoulder.

"Aunt Winnie?"

"Do you see that man? Over there?" Winnie gestured to a spot in the crowd, but all Portia saw was a wriggling mass of humanity.

"Who?"

"I think it's someone I knew years ago. I need to go." She hurried away without saying goodbye.

Portia watched her aunt walk away, wishing she had words that could call her back, words that could unlock whatever secret Winnie was hiding. No matter how much her aunt might say she was fine, Portia knew the truth. Something had changed the night Portia had announced that Howard had bought Celtic Seasons from Lester Connolly. Winnie hadn't been the same since. The reason why was just one more mystery Portia was determined to solve. She loved her aunt too much to do anything else.

"You're deep in thought." Mick's voice came from behind her, deep and rich and all too welcome.

Portia turned to face him, her breath catching in her throat as she met his eyes. His gaze drifted from her loose hair to the thick layers of gauzy skirts that fell to her ankles, then back up to her face. "The outfit is cheerful, but your expression is anything but."

"I was hoping bright colors might lift my mood, but they haven't."

"Then maybe I'll have to do something to try and change that. Which way are we headed?"

"The ring-toss booth."

"I know where it is. Let's go."

"There's no need for you to come with me. I'm sure I can find it."

"It's not a problem. I'm heading there anyway." He grabbed her hand, walking with her toward the lights and activities set up on the church lawn. The warmth of his touch spread through her glove and up through the thick turtleneck she wore. Or maybe it wasn't his touch, but his presence that warmed her. She wanted to lean her head against his shoulder, tell him all the things that were worrying her, ask him for advice.

And that would be a big mistake. Spending time with Mick was bad enough, counting on him was like asking for another broken heart. She bit her lip, tried to focus on something other than her longing to trust a man who seemed too good to be true. "Is Katie with you?"

"No, she's home tonight. My friend won't be in until late and I didn't want her out without me."

"You're here. Couldn't she have stayed with you?"

"I'm volunteering. I didn't think that would be much fun for her. Mom offered to let her have a slumber party at her house, so I think Katie's okay with the change in plans."

"Have you told your mother what's going on?"

"Yes. Both of my parents know about the threat."

The ring-toss booth was up ahead, a wooden structure with a large diamond ring painted on the side. "It looks like we're here. Thanks for walking me over, Mick."

"Walking you *and* myself over. Did I forget to mention that you and I are ring-toss partners for the next couple of hours?"

"You might have." She couldn't stop her smile, or the little thrill of pleasure that shot through her.

He eyed her, his gaze solemn and intense. "I'm surprised."

"By what?"

"You. I was sure you'd tell me you didn't need help at the booth."

"I've worked this booth three years in a row. It gets crazy. There's no way I'd ever say I didn't need help. Though I am kind of curious about how you managed to get assigned with me. Trisha Smith has worked with me all three years."

"Yes, but Trisha doesn't have friends in high places and a mother who is on the Winter Fest planning committee."

"Your mother booted Trisha out of her favorite assignment so you could take her place?"

"It was for a good cause."

"Oh, so now I'm a cause?"

"No, you're a beautiful woman who may not realize just how much danger she might be in. Think of me as an insurance policy. You probably won't need it, but if the time comes and you do, it's worth every penny you spent on it."

"Every penny? Should I expect a bill?"

"Not yet. Maybe in fifty years."

Fifty years. As in a lifetime. As in what was happening between Portia and Mick was way too much, way too soon. "I appreciate this, Mick, but I really don't need a bodyguard."

"Maybe not, but everyone can use a friend." He smiled again and Portia's heart did more than flip. It did a happy little jig. That wasn't good. Not good at all. Mick Campbell wasn't like any of the other men she'd known and not like anyone she'd ever dated. He was better, more decent. The kind of man people depended on. But Portia couldn't allow herself that luxury. Sure, Mick seemed to be dependable and trustworthy, but so had Tad. Or, at least, she'd wanted to believe he was.

The truth was a little more complicated and a lot more difficult to swallow. She'd sensed that Tad wasn't as committed to their relationship as she'd been. She just hadn't wanted to admit it. After all, there'd been Jasmine to consider; an eight-year-old without a mother.

And Mick had a six-year-old daughter who didn't have a mother.

No, hanging around with Mick was not a good idea.

She glanced at him, saw that he was watching her with dark, intense eyes. "What?"

"Just wondering what's put that frown on your face."

"I'm not frowning."

"Could have fooled me." They'd reached the ring-toss booth and Portia moved into place behind the counter, trying not to meet Mick's eyes as the person she was replacing explained the game and passed her a tub of prizes. Two hours. She and Mick were going to spend two hours together. And in that time, Portia had to do everything in her power not to fall for the man.

Too late. You're already falling.

She ignored the nagging little voice in her head and got to work. It wasn't long before her duties were in full swing as she attended to the children and young adults standing in line to try the ring toss. Excitement and laughter filled the air and soon her tension eased and she was laughing, too, smiling at the antics of the youngest children and helping them as they attempted to win prizes.

She put her hand on one little boy's, guiding it as he tossed the ring. "There! You got it. Go ask Detective Campbell to let you choose a prize."

"Keep helping them win and we won't have any prizes left," Mick whispered, his lips so close to her ear she could feel their warmth. The memory of those same lips pressed against hers flashed through her mind and Portia's heart did the same telltale jig it had done before.

She stepped away, clearing her throat and trying to

look completely unaffected. "That might not be so bad. If we run out of prizes, we'll get to close the booth and go inside where it's warm."

"You're cold?

"Aren't you?"

"I'm used to being outside in this weather. Here—" He put a hand on each of her arms and rubbed briskly. "Is that better?"

"Mick—"

"Relax. I'm just a friend helping a friend."

"And was that what you were being when you kissed me?" The question was out before she could think better of it and Portia's cheeks burned.

"No, but I get the feeling you think things are moving too fast between us. I figured I'd give you the time you needed."

"I… Thanks." What else could she say? Time was exactly what she needed, friendship was all she should want. So, why did his words steal some of the enthusiasm she'd had for the evening?

Because she was fickle and foolish and didn't know what was good for her, that's why. She needed to get herself together and do it fast, before she did something she'd regret. Like telling Mick that time was the last thing she wanted. "Do you mind keeping an eye on the booth while I go get some hot chocolate?"

"No problem." If he suspected she was running from him, he didn't say as much, just released his hold on her arms and let her walk away.

Mick wanted to go after Portia, find out exactly what she was thinking. She'd seemed surprised by his announcement. Maybe even disappointed. He had to admit he'd been pleased by her reaction. She might

be going back to New York soon, but he had a feeling
Portia was going to play a big part in his and Katie's
future. He'd been worried by that a few days ago, but
now it filled him with the kind of anticipation he hadn't
felt in years.

To his surprise, she did return, moving toward him
with a foam cup in each hand, her hair escaping the clip
she'd pulled it into and sliding over her shoulder in
thick, black ringlets. At first she seemed intent on making it back without spilling the hot chocolate, her gaze
on the ground, a frown of concentration between her
brows. Then, as if she sensed his gaze, she looked up,
her eyes meeting his, a half smile curving her lips. There
was warmth in her gaze and humor, as if she knew that
anything between them would be a mistake, but was as
helpless as he was to stop it.

"I thought you might like some, too." She handed
him a cup, her dark eyes probing his, as if seeking answers to questions she didn't dare ask.

And maybe that was for the best.

Years ago, when Mick had met Rebecca, he'd been
swept away by the emotions of it. Young and rash, he'd
pursued and married her with dogged determination. It
was only later that he realized how little he and Rebecca
had discussed, how few of her goals and dreams he
understood. He'd loved her, but over time had learned
that their ideals and values didn't mesh, that what he felt
was important meant little to his wife and what she
wanted seemed frivolous and self-serving to him.

He wouldn't make that mistake again.

Time and maturity had tempered him. This time, he'd
wait for God's timing, wait for what he knew about Portia
to match what he was already beginning to feel for her.

EIGHTEEN

A replacement volunteer arrived a few minutes before eight and Portia told herself she was glad to be leaving the ring-toss booth and Mick. Sure, she found him attractive, interesting, fun, but that meant next to nothing. Hadn't she already proven that her taste in men stunk? Mick's promise of friendship had seemed sincere, his easy, relaxed manner making her want to believe that they could be just that, but even while they laughed and chatted with each other and with the families and children who flocked to the booth, something had simmered between them, a deep awareness of each other that told Portia that friendship would never be all that connected them.

She grabbed her purse and smiled at the plump, cheerful woman who was taking her place. "Have fun."

"Oh, I will, dear. You go on and enjoy the rest of the evening." The woman's eyes sparkled with mischief as she glanced from Portia to Mick. "The volunteer fire department is sponsoring a carriage ride. Wouldn't this be a perfect night for it?"

Maybe. If she weren't trying to avoid being alone with Mick and if she didn't plan to search her father's office at Blanchard Fabrics. "It is, but I've got to head home. My grandfather hasn't been doing well."

"Oh, yes, I heard." The woman patted Portia's arm. "Perhaps another night."

"Perhaps." Portia smiled, backed up a few steps and got ready to make her escape. Mick seemed distracted, his attention on a group of teens who were vying for places in line. Now would be the perfect time to leave. "Good night. Good night, Mick."

She hurried away before he responded, determined to get in her car and drive to Blanchard Fabrics without having to explain where she was going or what she was doing. Not that she needed to explain to Mick, but she knew how he was. He'd ask and then she'd feel obligated to tell. And that would lead to a conversation Portia would rather avoid.

"In a hurry?" Mick was beside her before she hit the parking lot, his long-legged stride slowing to match hers.

"Not really."

"Then maybe we *should* try the carriage ride. Just as friends, of course."

She glanced his way and he grinned, his eyes flashing with humor.

"You heard?"

"How could I not? Ms. Snyder has one of those voices that carries."

"Isn't she an elementary-school teacher? I think one of my sisters was in her class."

"Miranda and I were both in her class. She's retired now, but she hasn't forgotten how to use her voice to its best advantage."

"She's sweet."

"And a matchmaker."

"There seem to be a lot of them running around this town."

"My mother for one."

"Aunt Winnie for another."

"Should we even try to fight them?" They were at the car and Mick leaned against the roof as Portia fumbled with her keys.

"Fight them?" She managed to open the car door, despite the fact that her heart was racing and her hand trembling. "I thought we were doing the friend thing."

"That doesn't mean eventually we can't do both. Look…" He put a hand on her shoulder, urged her to turn and pointed to the navy blue of the cloudless sky. "The sky is clear, the moon is out. It's the perfect night for a carriage ride."

His offer tempted her more than she wanted to admit, but a gibbous moon and a sprinkling of stars couldn't last. Reality would come rushing in all too soon. Better to avoid the dream and accept the reality. "I can't."

"Too bad." His finger hooked under the belt of her coat and he tugged, pulling her close. "It might be fun."

"It might be dangerous." The words slipped out and Mick chuckled, releasing his hold.

"Dangerous? You're not afraid to stick your nose into a murder investigation, but you're worried about going on a carriage ride with me?"

"There's danger and then there's *danger*." She smiled.

"True, but I think I'd prefer you experiencing a little danger with me than having you out searching for answers that might get you killed." He was leaning against the roof of the Bug again and looked for all the world as though he planned to stay there.

"Who said I was searching for answers?"

"So you're saying you're content to let me handle the investigation, that you have haven't done some searching on your own?"

"I've been looking for information about my mother." That was the truth, at least.

"That's what I'm worried about. There's a murderer on the loose, Portia. Until I find him, it would be best if you save the investigating for the professionals."

"I can't. If my mother is out there somewhere I want to know it."

"And if your father is a murderer?"

She winced at his harsh tone, but answered, "I want to know it."

"Then let me do my job. I'll find the answers you're looking for."

"I wish I could, but this is my life, my family. I can't leave it in someone else's hands."

Mick was silent for a moment, then he nodded. "Be careful, then. I wouldn't want anything to happen to you."

His words followed her into the car and rang in her ears as she pulled into Blanchard Fabrics, a small voice inside telling her she should heed his warning.

Unfortunately, she wasn't prepared to listen. If he'd been in her position, Portia felt certain that Mick would do the same thing as she would—pursue his own answers rather than wait for others to find those answers for him.

She sighed and pushed the door open. The parking lot was empty, the streetlights casting more shadows than brightness. Unease froze Portia in place, her eyes scanning the dark corners of the building. Mick *was* a professional. Maybe leaving things in his hands would be the best way to go.

But she'd been to the factory a thousand times as a

kid and had come at night when she was a teen. Tonight was no different than any of those times and she hurried to the door, the key in her hand. Above her, the indigo sky shone with a hazy greenish light. The air was still and cold, the only sound, her shoes clicking against the pavement. She shivered, pulling her coat tight around her throat and walking briskly, an odd, anxious feeling spurring her toward the building. She might have spent hours here as a child, but she hadn't been back in years. The pressure her father put on her each time he saw her at the factory made any effort to show interest in the family business difficult. She stepped inside the building and punched in the security code, sagging with relief when the system was immediately disarmed.

The place had been modernized in the past few years, but Portia didn't pause to catalog the changes, just hurried down the hall and into the office her father used. This, too, had changed. The furniture was lighter and brighter, with cleaner lines. She'd venture to guess the tasteful design had been Alannah's doing. One wall held a family portrait. Ronald and Howard presiding over Winnie and the rest of the Blanchard women. Portia had been ten when it was taken, but still remembered the day and the odd feeling she'd had that things were off kilter, that the portrait showed not a complete family, but something broken and ill-fitting. She yanked open the desk drawers, but couldn't find her father's daily planner.

Then she opened the first of several file cabinets, searching under *T* for Trudy, *W* for Wife or Westside Medical Retreat, the name of the sanatorium where Trudy had apparently received treatment, even *F* for Family, but could find no files that were of interest. If she knew what she was looking for the search would be easier, but she didn't and her father hadn't conveniently filed the information in an obvious place. Where would he have kept it? She'd assumed he'd been paying for Trudy's treatment at the medical center, could think of no other possible explanation for how her mother would have afforded an almost twenty-three-year stay in a sanitarium.

Unless Trudy's parents were paying. It was possible. Portia and her sisters knew nothing about their maternal relatives. Maybe it was time to find out more about them.

She rubbed the bridge of her nose, trying to think through all the possibilities, but her mind circled back to the same thing again and again—there was no way Ronald hadn't known his wife was alive. Somewhere there was proof of what Portia believed. She just had to find it.

The computer. That's where *she* kept important information.

She leaned over the desk, ready to boot up the computer and heard a scuffling sound from somewhere out in the hall. She froze, her ears straining to hear more, her heart beginning a quick, frantic rhythm. There was another shuffling sound and a quiet click that made Portia's heart jump and her senses spring to attention. The sound could have been the scuff of feet on the tile floor, an arm brushing against the wall as someone moved closer to the office, or nothing at all.

It's a mouse or a rat. It's got to be.

But even as she tried to convince herself Portia reached for the light, turned if off and crept toward the door. Did she dare try to close it? She put her hand on the knob, ready to pull it shut and push the lock home.

"I know you're in here somewhere. Come on out and play." The voice was gruff, muffled and filled with malice, the sound of it so startling Portia jumped, nearly bumping the old-fashioned hat stand that stood near the wall.

Whoever it was came closer, his feet scraping against the floor. Portia imagined he was carrying a gun, a knife or some other horrible weapon in a gloved hand, while she stood paralyzed in an open doorway, waiting to be found.

Get yourself together and move!

The words roared through her mind and she slammed the door closed, her fingers fumbling with the lock. The door flew back toward her, slamming into her head with enough force to send her crashing to the floor. Stars danced in front of her eyes and she blinked them away, scrambling backward as a dark figure lunged toward her.

"You weren't trying to lock the door on me, were you? Something like that could hurt a guy's feelings." He grabbed her arm, hauling her to her feet and jerking her toward him. She could smell sweat and soap and something else. Alcohol?

Panic threatened, but she forced it down. If she were going to survive, she had to think and thinking meant keeping a cool head. "Who are you? What do you want?"

"What kind of question is that coming from a woman I just caught snooping through her father's office while he's gone?"

"I've got every right to be here. Let me go and get out." She jerked against his hold, but his fingers tightened, digging into flesh, rubbing against the bone until Portia was afraid it might break.

"Before we have some fun? I don't think so." He yanked her forward, so that she slammed into his chest.

"I said, let me go!" She stamped down on his foot,

heard him curse as his grip loosened and wrenched her arm from his grip. The door to her father's bathroom was a few feet away and she rushed toward it, her heart pounding so hard she could hear nothing else.

She almost reached the door. Almost. A hand fisted in her hair, yanked her off her feet. She went flying, stumbling backward and into the arms of her attacker. He spun her around, pushed his face into hers so that they were nose to nose.

"That wasn't very nice, lady." He panted the words, the stench of alcohol on his breath making her gag.

She didn't try to reason with him, didn't bother speaking again, just plowed into him with all her weight. He toppled sideways, curses spewing from his mouth as Portia raced into the corridor. She had to make it outside. Make it to her car. She'd accidentally left her cell phone there. She could call for help.

"That's it!" He caught the back of her coat just as she reached the door, spun her around and shoved her into the wall. Moonlight spilled in through the glass doors, flashing on something he held in his hand. A knife. Long and lethal-looking, moving toward her, pressing against the throbbing pulse in her neck. "I'm done playing. Move again and you die."

She didn't dare disobey, barely dared to breath and still the blade pressed inward, nicking her flesh. Blood seeped from the wound, trickling down her neck and into the collar of her shirt.

Please, God, don't let me die here.

The prayer whispered through her mind as the man leaned in close. She could see him now. Or at least see the ski mask he wore. Dark eyes gleamed out at her, rabid and inhuman. What he planned to do was written there and Portia knew if she moved she would die.

"You ready to cooperate now?"

Only until she found an opportunity to escape.

He must have taken her silence for consent. The blade pressed more deeply into her flesh, then eased.

"I thought the knife might be convincing."

She tensed, ready to jerk from his hold, but the blade flashed in the light, the tip suddenly resting just below her eye. "Be a shame to cut up such a pretty face, but a guy's gotta do what he's gotta do. You run again, I slice your face. Got it?"

She didn't dare move, didn't dare speak, for fear the blade would slip and cut her from eye to chin.

"I'll take the fear in your eyes as a yes." He chuckled, the sound scraping against Portia's raw nerves. "See, fear is a good thing. It's what keeps us alive."

His free hand stroked Portia's hair.

"And a lovely lady like you is sure to want to live. So, I've got a job for you, a message you need to deliver. Tell your boyfriend that he'd better back off the McGraw case. If he doesn't, people are gonna start dying. Tell him that. Got it?" He pulled the knife away, grabbed her chin, gripping it in cruel fingers.

"Yes."

He stared at her, his gaze sliding from her face down her torso and back up again. "Sure would be a shame if something happened to you. Or to that cute little girl of his. Or to his ma or pa. You tell him I said so. Now, get outta here before I decide I want to give you more than a message." He yanked Portia closer, then shoved her toward the door.

For a moment Portia stood still, her mind blank, her

body shaking with terror. Then his words registered. Go? He was letting her go? She raced out the doors, ran down the stairs to the parking lot, sure she heard footsteps behind her, smelled sweat and alcohol in the cold night air. Was he behind her? Playing a game of cat and mouse, letting her go so he could capture her again? She jumped into the car, locked the door, tires squealing as she drove out of the parking lot.

She needed to call the police, report what had happened, but her hands shook so violently she didn't think she could drive the car and hold a phone at the same time. There was a fast-food restaurant up ahead. She'd stop there, call for help. The parking lot was well-lit and filled with cars and people. Still, she checked the locks on both the doors before she grabbed her phone, her hands shaking, her body trembling

Who should she call? Whose number did she know? She grabbed Mick's business card, dialed his number. She didn't think beyond that, didn't try to justify her choice further, just prayed he'd answer.

NINETEEN

Mick sped down Main Street and pulled into the parking lot of the fast-food restaurant where Portia had said she was parked, praying desperately that he'd find her there and safe. He hadn't gotten much information over the phone, but what she'd told him had been enough to send his heart racing. A knife-wielding attacker, another warning. Things were escalating, the time they had left to find the perp before he did more than threaten, ticking away.

Portia's car was easy to find, the green Volkswagen a bright spot in a sea of dark SUVs parked near the entrance of the restaurant.

He strode toward it, his gaze scanning the parked cars and the people. No one stuck out, but that didn't mean the person who'd attacked Portia wasn't there. She'd said he was masked, that he'd approached her at Blanchard Fabrics and that she hadn't recognized his voice. It wasn't much to go on, but Mick had officers out looking anyway.

He knocked on her window, saw her jump before she turned to meet his gaze, her eyes huge and dark in a pale face.

The door flew open and she scrambled out, throwing herself into his arms, her hands clinging to his waist. She was shaking violently.

"Thank goodness you're here. I've never been so scared in my life." Her shoulders heaved with sobs, her head pressing against his chest.

His arms tightened around her and he smoothed a hand down her hair. "Shhh. It's okay."

"You were so right. I should never have tried investigating on my own. If I'd just listened to you—"

"Let's just be thankful you're okay. You are okay, right?" He tried to pull back, to see if she had any injuries, but she tightened her grip.

Finally, he just scooped her into his arms and strode back to his SUV. By the time they reached it she'd regained control, her sobs subsiding, her grip on his shirt loosening. Mick slid her to the ground, brushed wild curls from her face. "You okay now?"

She nodded, but didn't speak, and Mick turned her so that the light from the restaurant fell on her face. There were red welts on her jaw, a large bruise on her forehead and a bloody scratch on her neck. Her skin, so pale it was almost translucent, felt clammy and cold to the touch. Mick dragged his coat off, throwing it around her shoulders and, zipping it up around her chin. "You're in shock. Get in the truck so we can get you warmed up."

His tone was harder than he intended, his anger at the man who had brutalized Portia spilling out.

She didn't seem to notice, just slid into the passenger seat and huddled there while he turned on the heater and called in to the station. The news there wasn't good. The men who'd been dispatched to Blanchard Fabrics had found it empty, the door closed, but not locked, the alarm system off. The man who'd attacked Portia was gone, the likelihood of finding him slim, the chance that he'd attack again too high for Mick's peace of mind.

Anger and fear roiled in his gut, but Mick schooled his voice as he ended the call and turned back to Portia. "I'm taking you to the hospital."

"No, don't. I'm fine." Her eyes were glassy and vague, her hair a tangled mess. She'd pushed her arms through the sleeves of his coat, but her fingers didn't show at the ends of the cuffs, and she looked lost amidst the heavy leather.

He pushed a sleeve up, found her hand and squeezed gently. "You don't look fine."

"But I am. A visit to the hospital will just be a waste of time."

He ignored her protests and pulled out of the parking lot, heading for Stoneley Memorial. Portia was going to be seen by a doctor, whether she liked it or not.

She must have known where they were going, but she didn't protest and that worried Mick. He glanced her way, saw that she was drumming a rhythm against her thigh, her eyes scanning the sidewalk as they passed as if searching for something. Or someone.

"Do you think you'd know him if you saw him?"

"Not unless he was wearing a ski mask and carrying a knife." She shot him a half-hearted smile. "But I feel like I've got to look anyway."

"We've got police officers out doing the same."

"Yeah, and there are only a few thousand tall, large-built men in Stoneley. I'm sure they'll have no problem at all finding the one that grabbed me." From her feisty tone, it was apparent she was recovering from her shock and her fear, and Mick relaxed for the first time since he'd received her frantic call.

"We might not get him tonight, but eventually we will. Count on it."

"I am."

So was Mick. The attacker's ever more desperate attempts to gain his attention and force him to stop investigating the McGraw case made no sense. Rather than drawing Mick's attention away, the slashed tires and tonight's threat against Portia only made Mick more determined to find the person responsible. There was no way the perp couldn't know that. So what was his point? What did he really want to accomplish?

It was something Mick had to determine. Fast. Only then would he have the key to solving the case.

He placed his hand over Portia's, stopping its jerking, tapping motion. "Did anyone know you were going to Blanchard Fabrics tonight?"

"No."

"You didn't tell your sisters? Your aunt? Your father?"

"I was going there to snoop, Mick. The last thing I would have done was tell someone in my family about it. The only person I even considered telling was you."

"If you're hoping the compliment will make me overlook the snooping part of what you just said, you're going to be disappointed."

Portia hadn't thought about it in those terms, though now that she did, it would have been nice if he'd ignored the bit about her snooping. "I'm just telling it like it is. I wanted to look for information about my mother and see if I could figure out where my father was yesterday. Blanchard Fabrics seemed like the right place to do it."

"Didn't I tell you that *I* would find the information you're looking for?" He practically growled the words, his jaw tight, his knuckles white against the steering wheel.

So, this was Mick Campbell angry. Portia didn't like it. She liked even less that she was the one who'd caused it. "I'm sorry."

"Sorry? You could have been killed." He pulled the car into the hospital's parking garage and turned to face her. "The person who did this planned it out, was probably watching you and waiting for an opportunity. And you handed it right to him."

Watching her? Portia thought of the moment in the alley and the one up on the cliffs with Grandfather, the strangely shifting shadows, the flash of white that could have been a face.

"I see you understand what I'm saying. In the alley, on the cliffs the night of the storm, he could have been both places. Tonight you gave him the perfect opportunity to follow through on what he's been planning and if he'd meant you any real harm, I might be looking at your body on a coroner's slab rather than sitting here discussing things with you."

Portia shook her head, wanting to deny what he was saying. "Why? Why would he be following me? If this is about the McGraw case, then he'd be going after the people in your life, not going after me."

"You *are* one of the people in my life. Think about it. We were talking before the carriage ride the night you thought someone was in the alley with you. If he was watching me then he would have seen us together."

"But on the cliff—"

"There *was* someone there. All I can figure is the guy

had your house staked out, was waiting for his opportunity and planned to take it that night."

"Only, you showed up."

"Yeah, and I would have been with you tonight if you'd told me what you planned."

"You would have tried to talk me out of it."

"Maybe, but if your course was set, I wouldn't have let you go alone." He flashed her a crooked smile and turned off the engine. "Come on, let's go see the doctor."

Portia didn't argue. Guilt ate at her. Guilt over searching her father's office. Guilt over not telling Mick what she had planned.

"Listen, Portia," he'd come around to her side of the SUV and opened the door "After we're done here, I think you should pack your bags and go back to New York."

"I'm not supposed to leave until Friday. Winnie will be disappointed if I cut my visit short."

"I think she'd rather have you in New York than dead."

Dead? She really didn't believe it would come to that. If her attacker had meant to hurt her, he would have. Even so, maybe going back to New York was the best thing she could do, but it didn't feel like the right thing. Her family was in crisis, her grandfather's health failing, her father under investigation for murder. She couldn't leave Miranda and Aunt Winnie to deal with it all.

"I can't go. My family needs me."

"Your sisters are going, aren't they? Nerissa, Cordelia, Bianca, Juliet. Aren't they all leaving?"

"But Miranda can't and neither can Aunt Winnie. Someone needs to stay for them and I'm the one with the least obligations. I can take time off from my career without hurting it." And without missing it. Much as she might once have thought she'd find fulfillment in the career she'd chosen, she'd learned that success didn't always equal contentment. As the store had grown, as the class rosters had grown, as small galleries had begun to show her paintings, Portia had felt more and more like a person walking a path simply because she was on it, rather than because it was taking her where she wanted to go.

It was here in Stoneley that she found satisfaction and in the past few days contentment had come in bits and pieces, found not in the Manor where she'd grown up, but with Mick, the one place where just being who she was seemed to be enough.

"Think about it, okay?" He stopped before they walked into the hospital, his hand on her cheek, his eyes staring into hers as if he could see her very soul.

"I will."

"Good, because I've got some plans that might be difficult without you."

"Plans?"

He nodded, ushered her into the emergency room. "Carriage rides, sunsets and beautiful horizons."

Portia's heart skipped a beat at his words, at his tone. "I thought you said you didn't want to rush me, that friendship is good enough for now."

"I did and it is. But tonight I remembered something that I'd almost forgotten—time is too precious to waste."

"But—"

"You'd better sign in. It looks like a full house in here tonight." His words were casual, his demeanor relaxed, as if he hadn't just tilted Portia's world.

She signed in at the front desk, filled out forms, handed over her insurance card, all the while wondering what plans Mick had and how big a part she played in them. And how big a part she wanted to play in them.

She felt shaky and unsure as she took a seat beside him in the waiting area, her head pounding, her stomach churning. She'd wanted so desperately to know where God wanted her, what He wanted from her. Now, it seemed she was being offered something *she* wanted— a man of strong convictions and strong faith, one who seemed to care about her for who she was rather than what she might do for him.

Was Mick's presence in her life a God thing, or a Portia thing? She hadn't taken the time to ask herself that question when Tad walked into her life. She'd come to regret it. Now, she wasn't sure she'd know the difference between the two.

"Relax. I'm not planning our wedding, you know." Mick's quiet laughter rumbled in her ear, before his arm wrapped around her shoulders, pulling her close. "Just a few dates. Maybe a trip to New York this summer for Katie and me."

"I guess that doesn't sound so bad. Though lately I've been thinking New York isn't the place for me."

"Yeah? What is?"

"That's the part I haven't figured out yet. Sometimes I think Stoneley is it. There are so many things about it I love, even crave, when I'm in New York."

"So what's keeping you away?"

"The truth? My father. He's got this idea that my artistic talent would be better used at Blanchard Fabrics. I don't agree. If I lived here, I'd be fighting a constant battle to keep my independence."

"Only if you let yourself."

"It's not as simple as that."

"Isn't it?" He leaned back in his chair, the dark stubble on his chin softening the hard angle of his jaw.

"You're an adult who's built a great career for herself, built a life for herself. You don't have to answer to your father for the choices you make. You only have to answer to God and to yourself."

"I know."

"If you do, then you've got nothing to worry about. Ronald can only get under your skin if you let him. Speaking of which—" he gestured toward the door "—there he is."

To Portia's horror, her father was striding across the emergency room, scowling, Winnie, Miranda, Delia, Bianca, Juliet and Rissa close on his heels. None of them looked happy, all looked worried. Obviously, news of her exploits had reached them.

And apparently, Portia was about to experience the perfect end to the perfect day. She sighed, pasted on a smile and moved forward to meet them.

TWENTY

She survived her father's anger, his lecture, the embarrassment of having every female member of the Blanchard family squeeze into the examining room with her. What Portia wasn't sure she'd survive was knowing that news of her espionage-gone-wrong had probably spread from one end of Stoneley to the other thanks to Ronald's harsh, barking demand for an explanation and her own less-than-stellar response. Telling him the truth had seemed like the right thing to do at the time. In retrospect, it might have been better to wait until they were somewhere private to fill him in on the details.

If they hadn't been at the hospital with several witnesses nearby and Mick hovering next to Portia's shoulder, Ronald might have done more than snarl questions and stalk away, but even that had been enough to start tongues wagging. Since her return to the Manor, Portia had received at least half a dozen phone calls from supposedly well-meaning "friends."

Nosy neighbors is more like it. She stalked across the room, feeling antsy, angry and on-edge. She'd expected her father to confront her when she arrived home. Instead, he'd closed himself into his office and left Portia to stew in her own juices. It was an odd reaction, very un-Ronald-like, and it convinced Portia even more that her father had more knowledge about Trudy's whereabouts than he'd admitted.

"Portia?" Aunt Winnie peeked in the door, saw that she was awake and stepped inside the room. "I thought I'd come see if you needed anything."

"I'm fine." But she knew that wasn't the real reason Winnie was there and wasn't surprised when her aunt perched on the edge of the bed. Of all the people in the house, Winnie was the one Portia least wanted to disappoint and she braced herself for what was to come.

She was surprised when Winnie smiled. "I have to tell you something."

"What's that?"

"You should have told me what you planned on doing tonight. I could have saved you the effort."

"What do you mean?"

"Did you think you were the only one searching for answers?" Winnie smiled again, but it didn't ease the melancholy that had hovered around her for the past few days.

"You weren't snooping through Father's things, were you?"

"I'm afraid I was. Of course, I had the good sense not to go to the factory at night when it was empty." She stood and paced across the room. "When I didn't find anything, I confronted your father and asked him what he knew about Trudy. He denied knowing anything. Just as he did tonight when you told him why you were at Blanchard Fabrics."

"Do you believe him?"

"Do you?"

"No. I wish I could."

"I want to. I want it desperately. If he did know your mother was alive, the lie he told was unconscionable."

"Father has always lived by his own set of rules."

"Maybe so, but surely his rules didn't make it right to lie to his children, to keep them from their mother for so long. If they did, then I don't know my brother at all and I really don't know what else he is capable of."

"Aunt Winnie, we can't assume—"

"It's something we have to consider, Portia."

"I know." Portia wrapped the older woman in a tight hug, feeling slender bones and slight curves and realizing for the first time just how fragile her aunt was. "But that doesn't mean he's guilty."

"And *I* know *that*." Winnie squeezed Portia's waist and stepped out of her arms. Then, she touched the throbbing bump on Portia's forehead. "How are you feeling?"

"Like an idiot, but I'll get over it. I'm not sure the town of Stoneley will ever stop talking about my spying efforts against my own father, though."

"You'll be old news by next week. Now, I'm supposed to make sure you get home tomorrow. Will you be able to drive, or shall I try to get you an airplane ticket?"

Home? Portia's SoHo apartment, the busy pace of the city, seemed a lifetime away and someone else's dream. "I was thinking about going home, but Grandfather isn't doing well and I want to spend time with him while I can." And she didn't want to leave Miranda and Aunt Winnie to deal with whatever trouble was heading their way.

"That's sweet, Dear, and any other time I'd tell you that staying was a wonderful idea, but things being what they are, it might be safer for you to be in New York."

"I appreciate your concern, but what happened tonight wasn't about me. It was about the McGraw case. The person who did this wants Mick to stop investigating. I just happened to be a means to an end."

"Still, Mick says you've been asking a lot of questions. If you get too close to the person responsible, it's impossible to say what might happen."

"You've been talking to Mick about me?"

"He's concerned for your safety. And rightfully so."

"That doesn't give him the right to discuss things about me without my consent." Though she wasn't at all surprised that he had. Mick and Winnie attended the same church and clearly had more than a passing knowledge of one another's lives. He'd probably thought Winnie would be his ace in the hole—a surefire way of getting Portia to leave.

"You're taking this the wrong way. He called to ask how you were doing and we talked. It was as simple as that."

"Aunt Winnie, I'm not buying the innocent act. The two of you are in cahoots and it's not going to work. I'm not going home tomorrow. End of story."

"Your stubbornness isn't becoming." There was humor in Winnie's voice as she said it, her hazel eyes dancing with laughter. Portia's heart lightened at the sight, her worry about her aunt easing just a little.

"My stubbornness comes straight from your side of the family, so you can just tell Mick Campbell that I'm not going anywhere."

"I'm afraid you'll have to do that yourself. His mother and I are good friends. I wouldn't want to hurt our relationship by disappointing her son." With that, Winnie left the room, closing the door quietly behind her.

It was a setup. Portia could spot one a mile away and unless she missed her guess, Winnie's sole purpose was to get Portia to call Mick. Well, she was going to be disappointed, because there was no way Portia would fall into the trap. She leaned back against the pillows, closing her eyes and telling herself that she really *wasn't* going to call him.

Really.

"Oh fine. I'll call," she spoke to the empty room, her disgust with herself not quite outweighing her desire to hear Mick's voice. She used her cell phone, dialing his number quickly, her stomach tied in knots, her brain shouting that she was making a big mistake. It was one thing to let him call her, it was another to make a move toward him herself.

The phone rang once. Twice.

She hung up.

Chicken. Smart. She wasn't sure which adjective fit.

The deep intonations of Beethoven's Fifth symphony filled the silence and Portia nearly dropped the cell phone before she managed to answer it. "Hello?"

"You rang?"

Mick's voice rumbled in her ear and Portia sat up straight, her heart leaping, her stomach somersaulting the way it had when she'd been fifteen and had caught a glimpse of her first crush in the hallway in high school. "How'd you know?"

"Caller ID is a wonderful thing. What's up?"

"I heard you were talking about me."

"You make for interesting conversation."

"I'm sure the entire town of Stoneley would agree."

His deep, warm chuckle made her smile and she paced across the room, knowing she should be angry that he'd spoken to her aunt, but not able to find it within herself to be anything but happy to hear his voice.

"Maybe, but by next week you'll be old news and some-one else will be grist for the rumor mill."

"Funny, Aunt Winnie was just saying the same."

"She's right. So, are you planning to tell me off?"

"Because you told Aunt Winnie she should talk me into leaving tomorrow? I probably should. But I won't."

"Hmmm, interesting."

"What?"

"You. Here you have a great opportunity to put me in my place and you aren't taking it. I think that might mean you called me for absolutely no reason at all."

"I had a reason."

"Yeah? What?"

"I wanted to hear your voice" didn't seem like the right thing to say. "I wanted to tell you I'm not going home tomorrow, so your effort was wasted."

"Like I said, I'm growing on you."

"Like mold."

He laughed. "There you go. Did Ronald continue his lecture when you got home?"

"No, and that worries me."

"Why?"

"My father doesn't believe in backing down. Based on past experience, he should have been pounding on my bedroom door ten seconds after we arrived home, demanding more of an explanation. If he didn't, there's got to be a reason."

"Guilt?"

"That's what I've been thinking. It's what Winnie thinks, too."

"I've got some feelers out. We should know more about what happened to your mother and what your father knew about it soon."

"You think that will help you find Garrett's killer?"

"I think it will give you peace of mind." He paused, said something to someone, the conversation muffled. "Work's calling and I've got to go in a minute. We've had some new information come in."

"What?"

"The toxicology report on McGraw is in. He had low levels of alcohol in his system and high levels of an antidepressant. The combination of the two is what killed him."

"The poor guy. Are you sure—"

"That it wasn't an accident? We're sure. He's got no history of depression or anxiety and no prescription for the drug."

"But, he might have—"

"Portia, McGraw's biggest fault was that he thought too much about himself, that he thought he was untouchable. In the end, it was that which killed him."

"You said you were friends a long time ago. Maybe he changed."

There was a heartbeat of silence and then Mick spoke, his words carefully measured. "He didn't."

The words were final and Portia sensed that he would say no more on the subject, that maybe there were things he wasn't saying. It reminded her too much of the last conversations she'd had with Tad. The ones where she'd talked and he'd avoided. All the warmth she'd been feeling, all the connection with Mick fled and she gripped the phone with tense fingers. "I guess I'll take your word for it."

"Do me a favor, okay?"

"What?"

"Leave the investigating to me. At least for tonight."

"I can do that."

"Good. See you soon."

She disconnected, tossed the phone onto the bed and flicked off the light, then lay staring up at the ceiling. Mick was hiding something. There was no doubt about that. If she'd learned one thing from her relationship with Tad, it was how to read between the lines, how to interpret the pauses, the silence, the subtle shifts in conversation. How to know when she wasn't being lied to, but wasn't precisely being told the truth, either.

She told herself that Mick's secrets were his to keep, that they hadn't known each other long enough for her to care that he was hiding something from her. She just wished she believed it.

Maybe Mick and Aunt Winnie were right, maybe she should go back to New York in the morning. It would be the safe thing to do. In more ways than one. But she couldn't go, not with so many questions still unanswered and not if it meant leaving Miranda and Winnie alone.

"What should I do, Lord? Stay? Go?" she whispered the prayer, hoping for an answer. But there was no audible voice, no clear sign and all she could do was hope that whatever she decided wasn't a mistake. Sadly, based on her previous choices she felt pretty confident that it would be.

Mick grabbed the paperwork he needed for his meeting and glanced at the phone. He should call Portia back, tell her the truth about the past he'd shared with McGraw, about the promise he'd made, about the widow and children who might be hurt if people in town knew just how crooked his ex-friend was. She deserved to know, deserved to have a clearer picture of who McGraw was and why his murder wasn't nearly as surprising as it should have been. Only the promise he'd made to his former partner had kept him silent thus far. That and guilt over his part in McGraw's removal from the Portland police department.

The more he knew about Portia, the more Mick wondered if those reasons were good enough to keep her in the dark, but now wasn't the time to make a decision. Roy had called an emergency meeting and Mick had to be there. They'd be discussing the new developments in the McGraw case, the threats against Mick's family and the attack on Portia. Somewhere in the midst of the chaos, they hoped to find a common thread. If they did, they'd follow it to the source and find the person responsible. Mick's gut feeling was that everything that was happening was connected to the Blanchards, but he'd put aside those feelings for now, try to come at the evidence from a fresh perspective and pray that whatever he discovered wouldn't break Portia's heart more than it had already been broken.

TWENTY-ONE

"Are you sure you don't mind, dear?" Aunt Winnie eyed Portia with a mixture of worry and frustration. "I wouldn't normally ask, but I can't possibly leave Peg and Miranda to deal with father. He's in rare form today."

"Why don't I stay and help, too?"

"You've been cooped up in the house for two days. It'll do you good to get out."

"Then I don't mind filling in for you at church." Even if that meant answering questions she knew everyone in the community would want to ask. She'd spent the days since her attack tucked away inside Blanchard Manor. The departure of her sisters had only added to her sense of imprisonment. While she loved Miranda and Winnie, her oldest sister was practically a hermit who liked nothing better than to be sequestered in her room and her aunt was often so busy with charitable functions she didn't have time to sit and chat with a bored niece. Yes, it was definitely time for Portia to face the world. And if she chose the right clothes, she just might feel almost confident while doing it.

"Thank you, Dear. I really do appreciate this. Do

you remember Sarah Porter?" Aunt Winnie's voice broke into Portia's thoughts and she nodded.

"She owns the flower shop, right?"

"Yes, and she's also head of the Sunday school program. Just let her know you're taking my place and she'll show you where you need to be. I don't have time to call her."

A thump sounded from somewhere above and Aunt Winnie frowned. "That's got to be your grandfather throwing things again. I'd better go see if I can calm him." She hurried away and Portia grabbed clothes from her closet.

A modest wool suit, knee-high boots and a colorful scarf seemed perfect for looking the part of a mature, wouldn't-be-caught-dead-snooping-through-my-father's-factory woman. She doubted anyone would believe the facade, but it was worth a try.

The bruise was another matter entirely. Much as she tried to style her hair to cover it, it refused to be hidden. Finally, she gave up, patting translucent powder over the various shades of green and blue, pulling on her coat and bracing herself for whatever the morning outing would bring.

"You're leaving?" Miranda called from the second-floor landing as Portia strode across the foyer.

"Yes. Do you want to come?"

"I can't." Miranda didn't use Grandfather as an excuse and Portia worried that her words were all too close to the truth, that it was agoraphobia and her sister *really* couldn't leave the house.

"Why don't we just go to Sunday school together? That's only an hour. We'll be home before eleven." And it would be so good for Miranda to get out. Last year the eldest of the Blanchard sisters had taken a small part in Winter Fest. This year, she'd avoided it all together. Portia was sure that wasn't good, but felt helpless to do anything but suggest outings that her sister always refused to go on.

Today was no different. Miranda shook her head. "No. You go on ahead. I just wondered if you could pick up a few things at the store while you're out. The weatherman's calling for some major snow today and I want to make sure we have Grandfather's favorite tea stocked. It's one of the few things he still looks forward to."

"Sure. No problem." She walked up the steps and took the paper her sister held out to her, shoving it in her coat pocket and wishing she could reach out and pull Miranda out of whatever fearsome world she lived in. But she couldn't, so she just hugged her sister and stepped away. "I guess I'll see you later."

"Okay. Don't stay out too long. The storm is supposed to blow in around five. That little Bug of yours won't handle it well."

"Don't worry. I'll be home before then."

The sun bounced off the blacktop as she drove toward Unity Christian Church, the reflection almost blinding. She eased off the gas, her shoulders tense as she rounded a curve that hugged the cliff. This part of the road had always made her nervous, the thirty-foot drop and jagged, foam-flecked rocks below only partially blocked by railings. It wouldn't take much to lose control, to spin off the blacktop and over the cliff's edge. That's how the accident happened that caused her mother's death. Or so Portia had been told.

Now it seemed there was another story. One Portia could only begin to imagine. Despite knowing that Trudy suffered from postpartum depression, Portia couldn't believe her mother would have completely abandoned her daughters. She might not remember much about the woman who'd given birth to her, but she did remember a sense of comfort she'd felt in her presence. Long ago, her mother had loved her. Portia believed that. Which made it all the more difficult to believe that Trudy wouldn't have made some effort to get in touch with her girls. She might have been running away from the pressure of raising six young children, but that didn't mean she'd been planning to stay away forever.

Did it?

Was it possible Trudy *had* run away and never looked back? That for twenty-three years she'd been alive, living a life that didn't include her daughters?

Portia had come to Stoneley for answers. It didn't seem she'd be getting them. At least, not yet. Mick had told her he'd find them, had said he wanted her to have peace of mind about the matter, but she hadn't heard from him since she'd been attacked and had refused to give in to temptation and call. Which left her father, a man who was as determined to keep his secrets as Portia was to uncover them.

If only she knew how to do it.

Her thoughts didn't ease the tension she'd been feeling and she pulled into the church parking lot with a headache and a sense of dread she couldn't shake. Despite her need to escape the Manor, she felt almost afraid to step out of the car. Two nights ago, someone had held a knife to her throat. It could have been anyone. Maybe even someone she knew. Someone who attended Unity Christian Church.

"That's enough paranoia." She mumbled the words

as she stepped out of the Bug, the Sunday school materials her aunt had given her clutched in her hands.

"Do you make a habit of talking to yourself?" Mick spoke from behind her and she turned quickly, nearly losing her grip on the box, her feet slipping.

He grabbed her arm, holding her steady.

She caught her breath and her balance before she dared answer his question. "Only when I'm having a bad day."

"Then I guess I can assume this is a bad day." He pulled the box from her hands. "Maybe Katie and I can make it better. We're going for ice cream after church. Want to join us?"

"Ice cream in this weather?" Portia smiled at Katie who stood next to Mick, her red-gold hair tied into pigtails. "Was that your dad's idea?"

"It was mine. I went a whole week without talking out of turn in class and Daddy said that was cause for celebration." Her eyes sparkled with excitement, her cheeks pink from the same.

"I wish I could, but I promised I'd bring a few things home for my sister. I don't want to keep her waiting too long."

"There's a store right near the ice cream place. We could go there together, too, right, Daddy?"

"Katie, Ms. Blanchard doesn't have time. Maybe another day."

Katie looked crestfallen, but nodded anyway. "All right."

Portia knew she should leave it at that. In light of her feeling that Mick wasn't being totally honest with her, getting more involved with the Campbell family was at the top of her things-*not*-to-do list, but seeing the little girl so disappointed reminded her of her own childhood and all the times she'd been disappointed by her father's lack of interest in her life.

Could it really hurt to spend an hour making a little girl happy?

"You know, maybe an ice cream *would* be nice."

"Really?" Katie's face lit up, her freckled cheeks flushing with pleasure.

"Yeah, really. Why don't I meet you out here after the service and follow you to the ice cream shop? Then I can stop by the store and go home right after that."

"Yay!" Katie's squeal of joy echoed across the parking lot.

They stepped into the church together and Katie ran over to a friend, her excitement adding more bounce to her already bouncing steps.

"You made her day," Mick spoke quietly. "She's been talking about you non-stop since we had dinner together. The bracelet you helped her make was the highlight of show-and-tell Friday."

"I had fun helping her. She's got a good eye for someone so young." She hoped her voice matched his casual tone.

"I'll tell her you said so." He raised the box a few inches. "Where are we headed with this stuff?"

"I'm filling in for my aunt today. I'm just not sure which class she's supposed to be teaching."

"Probably Katie's. Her regular teacher is out for a couple of months. There's a volunteer sign-up sheet outside the door. Let's see if Winnie is on it. Katie, come on. It's time for class." He strode along the hall-way, eyeing Portia with a mixture of amusement and concern. "You've got quite a bruise on your forehead. Headache gone?"

"Mostly."

"I've been meaning to call and check in on you, but things have been hectic. Maybe we'll have a chance to talk over ice cream. There are some things we need to discuss."

"Developments in the case?"

"A few." He stopped in front of an open door, gestured to a piece of paper posted on the wall beside it. "This is it, and there's Winnie's name. Looks like you're teaching Katie's class."

"You're my teacher today? Yay!" Katie skipped into the room and Portia followed, Mick close behind.

She tried to ignore him as she unloaded materials from the box but it wasn't easy to do. Especially not when he stood against the wall, his gaze following her around the room, his eyes seeming to take in every detail of her appearance.

Heat crawled up her neck and she finally turned to shoo him from the room. "We're fine here, Mick."

"Is that your gentle way of saying get lost?"

"More or less." She grabbed crayons from the box. "It makes me uncomfortable when people stare."

"That's what you think I was doing?"

"What else?"

"Studying your outfit. I was trying to figure out who you were today."

"Yeah? And who did you decide on?"

"My best guess? A woman who would never consider snooping through her father's business office."

He was so close to what she'd been going for with her look that Portia laughed, all the tension and awkwardness she'd been feeling gone. "What gave it away?"

"The wool suit. Though I've got to say, those boots

don't quite go with the theme and the scarf almost threw me."

"Even a non-spying kind of woman has got to have *some* color. So, are you sticking around?" She half hoped he would. The other half wanted him to leave before she forgot what it was that had made her believe he might not be telling the truth.

"I was thinking about it." He pulled a few packs of crayons from the box. "But I'm also thinking that is exactly what your aunt Winnie was counting on."

"You think she set this up?"

"She and my mother are two peas in a pod. Matchmakers to their very core. As a matter of fact, I wouldn't be surprised if they collaborated on this."

"You might be right, but Aunt Winnie did have a good excuse for staying home. Grandfather's having a really bad morning."

"Yeah? What's up?"

"He's convinced someone is out to get him." She set coloring pages out and called the children already in the room to come to the table. "I guess it's just all part of the disease."

"My father-in-law went through it. I know that doesn't make it easier to accept."

"No, but thanks for trying to help. I guess I'd better get started before these kids get completely wild on me."

"And I guess I'd better go ahead to my own class. If people see us in here together they'll start thinking conspiracy—the two of us collaborating against your father."

"That is exactly what I don't need. I've already created enough of a stir on my own to keep tongues wagging for ten years. Add you to the mix and it'll be twenty more years of explaining."

"We couldn't have that. Of course, if you want, we can create another kind of stir. Give the good people of Stoneley something new to talk about." Mick leaned toward her, his gaze dropping to her lips.

Was he going to kiss her right there in church in front of his daughter and her friends? In front of anyone who walked by and cared to look in the room? And did she want him to?

Yes!

No!

Maybe.

He took the choice out her hands, backing up, smiling that slow smile that always made her knees weak and walked out the door.

She was relieved. She really was.

Sort of.

Sunday school passed quickly and Portia found a seat at the back of the sanctuary for the service. She wanted to concentrate on the sermon, but her thoughts kept drifting back to Mick. Today, he had seemed completely open and unguarded, not like a man who had secrets. He'd said he had things he needed to tell her, things that had to do with the McGraw case, but he hadn't even hinted at what they might be. Good news or bad? Proof that her father was guilty of a crime? Or proof that he wasn't?

No, if it were that kind of information he would have called her, not waited until a chance meeting. Or would he have? As much as she felt a connection with Mick, she didn't know him well enough to say.

"Do not worry about tomorrow, for tomorrow will worry about itself. Each day has enough troubles of its own." The pastor's words finally penetrated the fog of

Portia's anxiety and she sat up straighter, her mind fully focused for the first time since she'd entered the church.

Worry. Her favorite pastime. And hadn't it gotten her into more trouble than it had gotten her out of? She said she believed that God was in control, but when push came to shove, she spent more time worrying than she did praying. Somehow she'd forgotten God's promise— that He was in control, that every moment of her life was in His hands.

Lord, forgive me for not giving my troubles over to You sooner. I know that you're in control and that I have to get out of Your way and let You do what You will. Please help me do that. Strengthen my faith and give me the courage to face whatever the future holds.

Portia stood for the final hymn, a sense of peace filling her soul. She didn't know what the next few days or weeks would bring, but she did know that God was bigger than any problems or troubles she would encounter. With His help, she could make it through anything. She could only pray that her family would survive as well.

TWENTY-TWO

"Portia!" Mick strode toward her as she stepped out of the sanctuary, Katie close by his side.

She smiled down at the little girl. "Hey! Ready for ice cream, Katie? I'm thinking hot fudge."

"Daddy says we can't do it today. He's got an emergency."

"I'm sorry to hear that." Portia shot a look in Mick's direction. "Is everything okay?"

"Shots were fired at a convenience store outside of town."

"That's terrible. Was anyone injured?"

"Two people. Both should survive, but we've got to get the perpetrator before he shoots someone else. My boss wants me in on the investigation. Come on, Katie, we've got to hurry."

"Who's going to watch me while you're gone? Grandmom and Granddad?"

"No, I've already asked them one too many times. We'll call someone else. Maybe Erin from down the street. Or, Mrs. Carpenter."

"Not Mrs. Carpenter. She doesn't believe in TV." The slight whine in Katie's voice matched her unhappy frown, but she didn't say any more as Mick rushed her through the crowded fellowship hall and out into the winter day.

Portia kept pace with the pair, knowing she should be happy with the change in plans. After all, staying away from Mick and his daughter was probably the best thing she could do for all of them.

Katie's downcast expression and Mick's harried sigh as he pulled open the door to the SUV kept her from that happiness, and she put a hand on Mick's shoulder, stopping him before he got in. "I could watch her for you."

He looked surprised, then pleased. Then shook his head. "I couldn't ask you to do that."

"You didn't ask. I offered."

"Please, Daddy. We'll have so much fun together, won't we, Portia? And I won't even talk that much."

"Sorry, Katie, but Portia has errands to run."

"I can go to the grocery store, grab what I need and be at your house in a half hour tops."

Mick looked as if he was going to refuse again, then he shrugged. "If you really don't mind, it will make my life a lot easier and Katie's day a lot happier."

"I don't mind. I'll call my family and say I'm running late."

"And I'll call Nate and tell him to meet me at the house."

"Nate?"

"My friend from Maryland. I think it would be good if he was at the house with you and Katie."

The bodyguard. Portia nodded. "If you want him there, that's fine by me."

"Thanks. Here's my address." He scribbled on a piece of paper and held it out to her. "I'm just three doors down from my folks, so if you have any trouble with Katie they're close at hand."

"I won't. The two of us are going to have a blast. I'll be there as soon as I can."

"I really do appreciate this." He cupped her jaw and gave the good people of Unity Christian Church something to talk about.

Warmth spread through her driving away the winter chill. She wanted to burrow closer, steal more of his warmth. Stay right where she was forever, kissing him.

When he pulled back, Portia looked into his eyes, lost herself for just a moment in the fantasy of what-ifs—what if Mick was exactly who he seemed to be? What if she could step out in faith and trust God to give her what was best for her?

What if she were much braver than she felt when she looked at Mick and his daughter?

He drove away and Portia ran to her car, pushing aside her chaotic thoughts. She was going to spend some time with Katie, watch the little girl while Mick worked. She'd let God take care of everything else. After all, the past was the past. Dating Tad had been nice, but even at the beginning, their relationship had been more comfortable than exciting. She'd thought they'd had shared values and shared goals and Portia had thought that was enough to build forever on. By the time she'd realized the truth it had been too late, her heart already firmly entrenched in the dream of family, love and belonging.

She shook her head and pulled out of the church parking lot. She'd learned from her mistakes but she wouldn't let them determine her future. What happened with Mick was in God's hands, and the best thing she could do was allow Him to work it out in His way and His time.

By the time she pulled up in front of Mick's well-kept Cape Cod, most of her nerves were gone and she was ready to spend a fun afternoon with Katie. Then she met Nate O'Connor. The man looked exactly the way Portia imagined a retired cop should look—salt-and-pepper hair cropped short around a tan, lined face, dark eyes that speared into hers as she stood on Mick's front porch juggling bags and trying not to drop the ice cream and toppings she'd purchased.

"I'm Portia Blanchard. Mick's expecting me."

"Can I see some I.D.?"

"Maybe you could take one of these bags and I could get my I.D. out."

He seemed disinclined to do as she suggested, just stood staring at her, his expression unreadable.

"Mick *did* tell you I was coming?"

"Your family owns Blanchard Fabrics."

"That's right." Maybe they were finally getting somewhere.

"Mick's investigating your family."

"He's investigating a murder."

Nate grunted, pulled one of the bags from her hand and started rifling through it. "What's in here?"

"Ice cream and toppings." She pulled her wallet from her purse and held it open so he could see her license.

He nodded and took the other bag from her arms.

"That one is just bananas and more ice cream and toppings. Nothing poisonous, sharp or explosive."

He looked up from his search, flashed a crooked grin and stepped out of her way. "Sorry. Force of habit. Mick and Katie are getting changed. Wait here while I put the ice cream away."

The house was decorated in warm hues—butter-yellow walls, oak floors and rust throw rugs. A piano stood against one wall, pictures of Katie at various ages lined up on its lid. In one, a stunning strawberry blonde smiled down at an infant.

"My wife with Katie. It's one of the few pictures I have of the two of them together." Mick stepped up beside her.

"She was beautiful."

"She was."

"Do you still miss her?"

"It gets easier." Mick ran a hand over his hair, wishing he had time to say more about his relationship with Rebecca. Wishing he had more time, period. "I've got to head out. Thanks again for doing this."

"You've done plenty for me and my family. Consider this payback."

"I'd rather consider it friendship."

Her eyes widened and she smiled. "So we're back to that?"

"That and more. Aren't the best relationships built on friendship?"

"I wouldn't know."

"Then I'd say you're about to find out." He resisted the urge to kiss her again as he had in the church parking lot. That had probably been a mistake, but Mick couldn't regret it. Later they'd talk, but for now he had to go. "I'll be back as soon as possible. My parents' phone number is on the fridge. They'll be home by four. If I'm not here by then, give them a call. They won't mind filling in for a while."

"That won't be necessary. I already spoke with my

aunt and Miranda and told them I'll be home late."
Portia took off her coat and laid it over the arm of the
couch. The suit she wore skimmed a slim figure, her
boots and scarf adding high style to something that otherwise might have been plain. Somehow Portia made
the outfit look both effortless and well thought out.

"Portia! You're here." Katie rushed into the room, her
eyes dancing with excitement, a bucket of beads in her
hands. "I got all my beads out. Grandmom gave me
some new ones and a whole jewelry-making set."

"Slow down, Katie. Portia's barely gotten in the door."

But Portia seemed as excited as his daughter, kneel-
ing down to finger through the pile of supplies Katie had
set on the floor. "These are great. We can do something
really fun with them, but first, I've got everything we
need to make ice cream sundaes."

"You did? Ice cream! Can we have sundaes, Daddy?"

"Lunch first. Mr. O'Connor brought pizza."

"Pizza, too? This is going to be the best day ever.
Bye, Daddy." She threw her arms around him and Mick
held her close, wanting to memorize the sweet scent of
baby shampoo, the softness of her hair and the wiggling
urgency of her energy.

"Be good."

"I'll try. You be careful." It was what they said to each
other each time he left and he smiled, watching as Katie
raced into the kitchen.

"You two have a great relationship," Portia spoke
quietly, her gaze following Katie's progress, her expression melancholy.

"For now. We'll see what happens as she gets older."

"She'll know you love her. That'll go a long way in
making things easier during her teenage years."

"You sound like you have firsthand knowledge."

"Firsthand knowledge of what happens when a girl doesn't." She straightened, walked to the front door and opened it. "You'd better go."

He wanted to stay, ask more questions, find out more about Portia's younger years. But she was right, he had to leave. "Don't let my daughter give you trouble."

"That sweet little girl? That's not possible."

Mick laughed and walked out the door. He expected Portia to close it behind him. Instead, she stood in the threshold, waving as he pulled out of the driveway. There was something about seeing her there, her dark hair curling around her shoulders, a smile curving her lips, that made Mick want to call Roy, tell him that he wouldn't be able to help with the investigation after all.

Maybe it was because lately he'd realized how much Katie longed for a mother. Or maybe it was because lately he'd realized how alone he felt. Sure he had family around, but something was missing and he knew exactly what it was. He missed having someone to talk to, to share hopes and dreams with, to laugh and argue with. To grow older with.

He'd avoided committed relationships since Rebecca's death. Taking care of Katie and raising her the way he'd been raised had taken top priority. His life had seemed too full to add anything else. Then Portia had skated into his life and everything changed. What had seemed full now seemed empty. What had seemed like too much was no longer enough.

And fitting a relationship, even a long-distance one, into his life didn't seem nearly as impossible as it once had. As long as that relationship was with Portia.

* * *

The storm hit at four, snow falling in puffy white flakes that danced in the air before coating the trees and ground. Katie ran from room to room, staring out the windows in undisguised glee, chattering about snowmen and potential school closings. Portia wasn't quite as excited about the darkened sky and snow that fell like rain from the clouds. Miranda had been right to warn her. The Bug didn't handle well in the snow. If the storm continued, she might have to stay with Mick, Nate and Katie. There was no way she planned on driving home in it.

"It's looking bad out there." Nate stepped up beside Portia and glanced out the living-room window.

"Yeah, it is. If it keeps up like this we'll have two feet by morning."

Nate nodded, but didn't speak again. That didn't surprise Portia. He'd been silent for most of the afternoon, pacing through the rooms, then settling in a chair for a few moments only to begin pacing again. Watching him had made Portia almost as antsy and anxious as he seemed to be.

"Can we go outside, Portia? Daddy always brings me out when it starts to snow." Katie stared longingly out the window, her face pressed against the glass, her body humming with energy and excitement.

Portia wanted to give in, take her outside and let her enjoy the beauty of the afternoon, but Nate met her eyes, gave a subtle shake of his head.

"No, Katie, I think we'd better wait until your dad comes home."

"But—"

"Portia is right," Nate cut in smoothly. "You wouldn't

want your dad to be disappointed that you went out without him."

"He wouldn't be. He'd be glad I had fun."

"We'll wait anyway." Nate's words were gruff, his gaze scanning the dark yard as if he expected trouble.

Portia's heart started a slow, heavy thud, her nerves jumping to attention. "Is everything okay?"

"Fine. How about you take the kid into the kitchen for some hot chocolate?"

"Sure. Come on, Katie." But even as she ushered the little girl into the kitchen, Portia was glancing back at the living-room windows. How hard would it be for someone to break a window and gain access to the house?

Not hard at all. Maybe that's why Nate was pacing like a caged tiger. Maybe he was expecting someone to do just that.

Portia's pulse raced as she grabbed a mug from one of the oak cupboards, microwaved water and poured in a packet of cocoa that Katie provided. Then she set the mug on the table with a few cookies and returned to the living room. Nate still stood at the window, his shoulders tense, his jaw set.

"What's going on?"

"Something feels off." That he answered surprised Portia and she stepped closer, staring out into the gloomy day.

"It looks quiet to me."

"Yeah. Too quiet." He raked a hand through his hair and leaned closer to the glass. "Or maybe I'm just used to city life. This quiet country living is about enough to have me seeing trouble where there isn't any."

"That's probably what it is."

His nod was curt, his attention back on the empty

street and Portia knew he didn't believe it. He sensed danger. But from where?

Glass shattered, sending Portia backward, a scream rising in her throat, but the sound hadn't come from the window in front of her. It came from the back of the house. Katie's shrill, terrified scream filled Portia with the kind of terror she'd only ever imagined.

"Katie!" She raced toward the kitchen, Nate at her side, his gun drawn, fury flashing in his eyes.

Portia didn't know what she expected to see, but the kitchen was empty of anyone save Katie, who stood near the table, the mug of cocoa shattered at her feet, her eyes wide and round and filled with horror.

"Are you okay?" Portia raced toward her, nearly slipping in the liquid on the floor.

"Someone was outside, looking in at me." She sobbed the words, her freckles dark against paper-white skin.

"Where?" Nate barked the words, turning toward the sliding glass door that led from the kitchen into the backyard. "The window or the door?"

"The door. I screamed and he ran away."

Portia put an arm around the girl's shoulder, dragging her backward away from whoever might be lurking outside. "We need to call—"

Something exploded into the sliding glass door, shattering it. Glass flew across the room, spraying onto the counter and floors, slashing Portia's skin as she dove to the ground, covering Katie with her body. Her hand slid in hot chocolate and glass, pain slicing through her palm. Then everything happened at once—another explosion, Nate collapsing in a heap on the ground, blood pooling beneath him, Katie's high-pitched shriek, a dark figure lunging in through the broken glass.

Portia dragged Katie into her arms, racing through the doorway and into the living room. The front door. She had to get to her car. Get Katie somewhere safe. Call someone to help Nate. The thoughts flashed through her mind as she ran.

Something slammed into the wall near her head and woodchips sprayed her face, but she kept running, the weight of the little girl nearly too much, her arms trembling, her legs shaking. The cool metal doorknob was beneath her hand, escape in reach. She sobbed pulling the door inward. A hand fisted in her hair, yanking her backward, pulling her off her feet. She fell hard, the breath leaving her lungs, her arms still locked around Katie. She pushed the little girl up and away, screaming as she turned toward their attacker.

"Run, Katie! Go to your grandparents."

That was all she had time to say. The intruder lunged, hazel eyes cold, clinical and more scary than Portia could have imagined possible. She struck out with a fist and hit his nose. She pulled back for another punch just as he reached for her throat, made contact, his gloved hand pressing hard. She saw stars, all air, all breath, every chance of life cut off as his fingers pressed harder.

"You go ahead and run, little girl. Go and leave your friend here to die. Or come back and I might decide not to kill her." The words were chilling, the hand tightening a fraction as Portia slammed an elbow into his ribs. She wanted just enough breath to scream at Katie, to tell her not to worry, that she'd be fine, but her lungs burned with the need for air and she couldn't force a sound past his ever tightening grip.

"Let Portia go!" Katie must have rushed in to attack. The man swayed, his grip loosening. Portia gasped for air, tried to block her attacker as he made a grab for Katie. He cuffed Portia in the side of the head, shoved her away and lifted the screaming girl.

"You're not taking her." The voice wasn't Portia's, the terror behind it rasping out in uncontrolled fury. She grabbed a lamp, praying for the strength to bring it down on the man's head. She swung hard, blackness still dancing at the edge of her vision. He ducked, pulled something from his waistband.

"Enough!" The words were a wild roar, the gun he held pointed at the still-struggling Katie. Portia froze, her hands trembling, her mind blank of all but one thought—that she had to do whatever it took to get Katie out of this alive.

"One more move, one more word out of either of you and you're both gonna die right here, right now. Understand?"

"Yes." Portia met Katie's eyes, tried to communicate a sense of calm she didn't feel, a sense of faith she couldn't grasp.

Katie's eyes were focused on the gun, her mouth a wide, silent *O*.

Don't move, Katie. Don't struggle. Portia wanted to tell Katie to hold still, to wait. Tell her that they'd find a way out of this, but she didn't dare speak, the wild-eyed look of the intruder telling her that he was on the verge of pulling the trigger.

"That's better. Now, we're leaving. All of us. Put the lamp down, lady, and let's go. You try anything and the kid gets the first bullet."

An image of Nate, lying in a pool of blood on the kitchen floor, filled Portia's mind and was eclipsed by another—this one of Katie's broken body lying cold and still in the snow. She dropped the lamp back into place and moved toward the front door, praying with all her heart that God would give her another chance to free the child.

TWENTY-THREE

The commotion started down the hall from Mick's office as he, Roy and Drew bent over a map of Stoneley and the surrounding area. He tried to ignore it, his focus on the task at hand—marking potential hiding places and designating areas to be searched. The description given by the wounded clerk and gas station attendant indicated that the shooter had been driving an older sedan. The car wouldn't do well in ice and snow and that was to their advantage. It was possible the perp had parked on a side road when the snow began. If so, their team would find him.

The commotion increased as Mick marked an old logging road and he glanced up at the closed office door. "What's going on out there?"

"I don't know, but I'm thinking I'd better find out." Roy stood, stretched his long, lean frame. "Maybe one of the patrol guys we've got out there has found our perp. It'd sure save us a trip out in this wicked storm if one did. And I, for one, wouldn't mind that at all."

He took a step toward the door, but it flew open before he reached it and Penny Simmons, dispatcher and long-standing fixture at the Stoneley police department, stumbled in. In the nine months Mick had worked there, he'd never seen her be anything but cheerful and calm. Now, her face was devoid of color, her eyes wide and filled with stark fear.

He stood, started toward her, not knowing what was wrong, but knowing whatever it was had to be big.

She grabbed his arm, her grip tight and hard, her knuckles white. "Mick, we just got a call in. There's been a shooting at your house. An ambulance is on the way."

"What?" He shrugged off her hold, raced toward the door, not waiting to hear more.

"Mick, slow down, man." Drew raced after him, shoving a coat into his hand. "You can't go out there half—"

"I'm going." He jumped into the SUV, barely giving Drew time to hop in the passenger seat before he tore out of the parking lot.

It took five minutes to reach the house. Five of the longest minutes Mick had ever lived. He beat the ambulance, but could see that the front door was open and someone paced the front stoop. Mick jumped out of the SUV.

"Mick!" His father raced toward him, specks of blood staining the white button-down shirt he wore, his face pale and haggard. "Thank God you're here. Katie's—"

"Is she hurt?" His stomach dropped, his world shrinking to that one moment, that one place as he shoved past his father and raced into the house.

"No, not hurt. Missing. I can't find her. Can't find her anywhere." His voice broke and Mick wished he had it in himself to offer comfort.

"What about Portia?" He glanced around the room, saw the tipped lamp, blood on the floor.

"Gone, too. Only Nate is here and he's hurt."

"Shot?"

"Through the sliding glass door and into his head. I was putting out bird seed and heard the shot. Didn't realize what it was until I heard the second one. If I had—"

"This isn't your fault."

"You don't understand, I came around the house after I heard the second shot, wanting to check on Katie. I saw the car pull out of the driveway."

"You have a description?"

"It was Portia's. The little green car. She wasn't driving it. If only I'd been a minute faster—" His voice broke again.

"It's okay. I'll find them."

Sirens screamed outside, coming closer as Mick strode into the kitchen. Blood was everywhere. Splattered on the wall and counter, pooled under Nate who lay on the floor. Hank Ingalls, Mick's next-door neighbor and a volunteer firefighter was applying pressure to the wound. He looked up as Mick entered the room. "Thank God you're here."

"How bad is it?"

"Near as I can tell it's only a flesh wound. Probably dug a gouge in his skull, but he should live."

"Nate?" Mick knelt beside his friend, hoping the ex-cop could offer something that would lead him to the person responsible. "What happened, buddy?"

Nate opened his eyes, shook off Jackson's hold and stood, weaving a little as he did, his hands pressing the blood-soaked towel to his head. "Guy shot right through the glass. Stupid mistake."

"His or yours?"

"Both. I should have known better than to make myself a target. But he should have planned a better way of getting rid of me."

"He got rid of you just fine. And got away with Katie and Portia. I've got to find them." Mick started back toward the front of the house, but Nate caught his arm.

"Wait. I got a look at the guy before he pulled the trigger the second time."

"He shot at you more than once?"

"Yeah. He missed the first time, caught me the second time as I was turning to get Portia and Katie out of the room."

"You can give a description?" It might not be much, but at least a description would give them something to go on.

"Easily. Get something to write on."

Fifteen minutes later, Mick was in his SUV praying hard and searching for any sign of Portia's car. An APB had been issued on Portia's car along with an Amber Alert. Local news stations were already airing the story, radio stations were announcing names and descriptions. But it wasn't enough. Not nearly. Mick gripped the steering wheel. Every minute that passed was a minute longer that his daughter and Portia were in the hands of a murderer.

"Mick, slow down, man. You get yourself killed and you'll be no good to your daughter." Drew had a white-knuckled grip on the door handle, but Mick suspected he was filled with rage rather than fear.

"The SUV handles well in the snow." He eased off the gas pedal anyway, knowing his panic would do Katie and Portia no good. "Don't worry, though, I've got no intention of dying before I get my hands on the man who took my daughter and Portia."

"We'll get him. I don't care if takes years."

"We don't have years." Mick snapped the answer, knowing he shouldn't take his fear and frustration out on Drew, but unable to keep his emotions in check. "Sorry. I'm on edge right now. Worse than on edge."

"I know. I'm with you, man. We'll find the guy and we'll put him behind bars for the rest of his life."

They rode in silence for several minutes, the snow falling in quick, fat flakes. Visibility was low, driving difficult. That had to be a good thing. No cars on the roads, nowhere for the perp to go. Portia's car wouldn't be able to hold the road in these conditions, which meant the guy who'd taken it would have pulled over, stopped somewhere to wait things out. Or maybe he'd just keep going until he ran off the road or made his destination.

Mick's cell phone rang and he grabbed it, his heart leaping, his mind racing through a million possibilities. "Campbell."

"Mick, we've got something." Roy's voice was rough, his words rushed.

"Tell me."

"The car involved in the convenience-store shooting. One of our guys found it parked a block away from your house."

"So the shooting was a set-up designed to get me out of the house."

"Seems that way."

"It worked."

"The perp knew we'd call you in on a shooting."

"He planned it all. So he must have planned a place to take my daughter and Portia. We just need to figure out where that is."

"Mick, this guy shot two innocent people. He probably killed McGraw. There's a possibility—"

"Portia and Katie are still alive. He won't kill them until he's got what he wants from me."

"Do you know what that is?"

"No." But when he found out, he'd give the guy whatever he wanted, say whatever he had to to get Katie and Portia back.

"We're dusting the car for prints. Maybe we'll get a match and put a name to our guy. And maybe that will give us some idea of where we can find him. I'll keep you posted." The line went dead and Mick tossed the phone into the console.

Daylight was fading, the storm gaining force and his daughter and Portia were out there with a madman. Mick's hands gripped the steering wheel, his heart slamming in his chest. He wanted to shout his rage and fear, but knew it would do no good. All he could do was pray that God would keep them safe because Mick didn't know what he'd do if they weren't.

Portia squinted out the window of the Bug, trying to see through the swirling snow. They were on a dirt road, heading for somewhere Portia was sure she and Katie wouldn't want to be. The man beside her sat forward in his seat, leaning over the steering wheel. He looked normal, pleasant, nothing like the cold-blooded killer she suspected him to be. He caught her eye, frowned. "You trying to memorize my features?"

"No."

"Good. Not that it'd do you any good anyhow." The car bumped over something, skidded to the side and the man cursed, barely able to steer the Bug back on course.

"My car isn't meant for this kind of weather."

"Your car is meant to do exactly what I want it to do. And so are you. Now, get that kid to stop crying or I'll give her something to cry about." He nearly shouted the last words and Portia turned to Katie, who huddled in the backseat, her sobs filling the small car.

"It's okay, Katie. We're going to be fine."

The little girl shook her head, as if she understood that they might not live through the night, but she stopped crying.

"Here we are. Home sweet home." The man pulled up in front of a log cabin, opened his door. "Out. Both of you." He gestured with his gun and Portia grabbed Katie's hand, tugging her out of the car with her.

"Where are we?"

"That's not something you need to worry about." He shoved her forward. "Get in the cabin."

Portia wanted to run, but knew she couldn't carry Katie far enough or fast enough to escape. Her heart thudded in her chest, her legs shaking with fear as she took one step after another toward the cabin. Katie clutched her hand and Portia could feel her trembling, hear her soft sobs and quiet gasps of fear.

She had to get her out of this alive. There was no other option.

Please, God, help me keep her safe.

The prayer whispered through her mind as their kidnapper opened the door, shoved Portia roughly forcing her inside. She stumbled but kept her grip on Katie's hand, afraid he might grab the girl and run.

The cabin was small. Probably used for hunting. Just one room. Rough-hewn with long plank floors, a cot, a dresser and a chair. Dirt and debris littered the floor and cold air seeped in through cracks in the walls. If there were windows they were boarded up and the only entrance seemed to be the door Portia had been shoved through.

"Enjoy your stay. It should be a short one." The door

slammed shut and the room went black. Portia expected to hear the car engine roar to life. Instead, she heard the kidnapper's voice, loud and rough, his words unclear. He sounded like he was arguing with someone, though Portia knew no one else was there. Had he made a phone call? To whom? His words faded away. Moments later, the Bug's engine roared to life.

"Is he gone?" Katie's voice sounded in the darkness, her fingers tightening around Portia's.

"I think so."

"That's good, then. We can get out and go home."

If only it were that simple. They were miles away from the last house Portia had seen, on a dirt road that had probably once been used for logging vehicles. Someone might eventually come this way, but waiting for help wasn't an option. It was cold, even inside the cabin. There was no way they'd last the night. "You're right. We're in much better shape than we were a minute ago. Let's go see what's outside."

She felt along the wall, found the door and shoved. It didn't budge. She tried again with the same results.

"What's wrong? Can't you open it?"

"No. I think it's stuck."

"I can help."

"No." The door had been locked from the outside, rigged somehow to keep them inside. Which meant either that the man was going to return, or he planned to leave them there to die. Portia didn't like either option. "Let's do something else instead. There was some furniture in here. Do you remember?"

"A…chair."

"And a cot and a dresser."

"And dirt. And probably bugs."

And maybe another way out. "Not when it's this cold. Let's check the dresser. Maybe we can find something useful."

"Like a phone?"

"That would be nice." But not likely. Portia should have tried to grab her purse and cell phone from the car, but she'd been too afraid their kidnapper would do what he'd threatened and shoot one of them. *It's okay. The situation isn't hopeless. Just stay calm and trust that God will help you get out of this.*

She cleared her throat, hoping that Katie couldn't sense her panic. "This cabin might be used for hunting. If it is, maybe there are clothes in the drawers. Or even food." She stripped off her suit jacket as she spoke, the silky camisole she wore beneath no protection at all from the cold.

"Here, Katie, put this on." She felt for the child's shoulders, draped the jacket around them.

"But you'll be cold."

"I'll be fine. Now, let's check those drawers."

As she'd hoped, they were filled with flannel shirts, thick wool socks, a lightweight jacket and jeans. Portia bundled Katie up as best she could, ignoring the child's protest about the musty and mildewy scent that wafted from the clothes. Then she pulled a pair of oversized jeans on under her skirt, threw two flannel shirts over her camisole and took Katie's hand once again, feeling along the wall, letting her fingers do what her eyes could not.

Finally, she found what she was looking for—a smooth plank of wood that gave a bit as she pushed.

"I think this is it, Katie. There's a window under this board. Stand over against the wall. I'm going to try to smash the board out."

"You're not going to leave me here, are you?" Katie clutched her hand, refusing to let go when Portia tried to tug away, her fear palpable in the darkness.

Portia pulled her into her arms, hugged her close for just a moment, smelling baby shampoo and hot chocolate and knowing she would do whatever it took to get Katie back to her father. "I would never leave you. We're in this together, but I've got to push this panel out so we can get outside."

"All right." Katie slowly released her hold and Portia could hear her move away. "But maybe you'll need my help."

"I will. You pray while I push."

"I can do that."

"Good girl."

The chair was sturdy and difficult to lift, but fear gave Portia strength and she slammed it into the plywood. Slammed it again. The third time, she felt the plywood give. The fourth revealed a sliver of grayish light. Finally, Portia put the chair down and shoved her shoulder into the barrier, feeling the crack and give as the board fell away.

"You did it!" Katie squealed in delight and threw herself into Portia's arms. "Now we can go find Daddy and tell him about that man."

"Yep, and I bet he's already out searching for us." She hoped and prayed he was. Prayed that Nate hadn't been killed, that somehow he'd managed to go for help.

Outside, snow fell fast and heavy, coating the ground and the trees that surrounded the cabin. Portia could see nothing but wilderness. No tracks. No houses. Nothing that would indicate they were within walking distance of help, but she'd paid careful attention to the landscape on the way here, knew that help was just a few miles away, down the dirt road and to the left.

Just a few miles. Easy. If it weren't snowing. If Katie weren't so small. If. If. If.

Have faith. Stop doubting. God has never failed you before and He won't now. Portia closed her eyes for just a second, listening to the still, small voice that told her everything was going to be okay. Then she smiled down at Katie, hoping the little girl didn't sense her fear. "How would you like to go on a sleigh ride?"

"A sleigh ride?"

"Yep. The legs on that cot look like they fold down. If they do, you can sit on it and I'll pull you."

"But what if they don't? You said you weren't going to leave me."

"If they don't, we'll break them off and I'll pull you. One way or another, we're getting out of here and we're going together."

TWENTY-FOUR

Forty minutes. The time shouted through his head and Mick grimaced. He knew exactly how much time had passed. The snow kept falling, covering tracks, making driving difficult and rescue efforts precarious. If the search were called off, Mick would continue. He had no choice.

The phone rang and he grabbed it, holding it to his ear as he maneuvered down one of the old logging roads at the edge of town. "Yeah?"

"We've got a print match on the car."

"Who?"

"Ex-con by the name of Richard Zimmerman."

"The name is familiar."

"It should be. You and McGraw nabbed him for carjacking nine years ago. Guy's wife divorced him and disappeared with their kids. He got out of prison two months ago. Looks like he decided it was payback time."

Mick remembered the case. He and McGraw had been off duty when they'd witnessed the carjacking. Their capture of Zimmerman and rescue of the victim had made Portland papers.

"There's more. And this may be good. We got a call from a landlord down in Milltown. One of his renters owns a car that fits the description of our perp's car. I had Milltown PD bring mug shots to the guy and he picked Zimmerman out."

"How long has he been renting in Milltown?"

"Six weeks."

"So he was in the area when McGraw was killed. We getting a search warrant?"

"I'm already on it."

"Anything else?"

Roy hesitated, then sighed. "I'm telling you this because if my daughter were out there, I'd want to know, but that doesn't mean you're going in. I've already called in state troopers. This is a hostage situation and I can't having you rushing in there without any thought to how things need to be done."

"Going in where?"

"If I tell you and you go and get yourself killed, or do something that compromises our case—"

"My daughter's out there. Do you think I won't go by the book, do everything I can to get her and Portia out alive?"

He heard Roy sigh, but when the other man spoke Mick knew he was going to get what he wanted. "Piney Orchard Road. A witness saw a green VW Bug heading west. Thought it was strange what with the heavy snow and all. I dispatched men to the area and they're in pursuit."

"They've got a visual?"

"Mick, you're not part of this. Stay away until we get the situation under control."

"Sorry, Captain, I didn't quite hear that." Mick threw the phone onto the dashboard, did a U-turn and headed back the way he'd come.

"What's going on?" Drew's voice was tight, his concern obvious.

"Portia's car has been spotted."

"Let's pray she and Katie are still in it."

They had to be. Mick refused to contemplate anything else.

By the time they reached Piney Orchard, the road was thick with snow. The SUV handled it easily, but Portia's car wouldn't be faring as well. Worry thrummed along his nerves and gnawed at his stomach. Zimmerman had spent nine years stewing in the juice of his rage. Now he was acting out whatever plan for revenge he'd concocted. Did he intend to take Mick's family the way he probably felt Mick had taken his? Every case he'd ever investigated flashed through Mick's mind—grisly murders, more than a few of the victims children. An image of Katie and Portia lying on coroner's slabs filled his mind and cold, clammy sweat beaded his brow.

"You okay?" Drew's voice pulled Mick from his morbid thoughts.

"Fine."

"Maybe I should drive."

"The guy we're after is an ex-con. McGraw and I nabbed him nine years ago. I should have listened to Portia when she said her family wasn't involved in McGraw's death."

"Everything pointed in that direction."

Mick shook his head. "It pointed in that direction because that's where we were looking."

"It wasn't the only direction we were looking. You were checking McGraw's clients. You can't blame yourself if Zimmerman's name didn't come up."

Please God, let them be okay.

He'd barely finished the prayer when he spotted the first police cruiser. Lights flashing, it sat at the side of the road. Another was just ahead. And another. Officers were running into the woods that lined the street. Black smoke snaked upward and Mick caught a glimpse of crushed metal and bright flames. "No!"

He slammed on the brakes, jumped from the SUV and raced into the trees just as an explosion rocked the world. It didn't stop him. He kept running, ignoring the hands that grasped his jacket, the shouts to keep back. The Bug was engulfed in flames, blackened and ugly against the white snow.

Something slammed into his back and Mick fell forward, fighting against the arms that held him down.

"Mick, buddy, it's too late. Anyone in the car is already gone," Drew shouted the words close to his ear and Mick bucked him off starting toward the burning wreck again, his heart beating a slow, horrible rhythm in his chest. He felt hollow, empty of everything as he took another step toward the car. Someone shouted from the road, the words not registering as Mick moved through the trees.

"Did you hear?" Drew grabbed him, pulled him into a bear hug. "Katie's okay! She and Portia are okay! A state trooper was on the way here and saw them walking out of an old logging road. He's taking them to the hospital."

It took a moment for the words to register. When they did, Mick turned and raced back toward the SUV.

People liked to talk. If Portia hadn't known it before, sitting in the triage room at Stoneley Memorial Hospital would have convinced her of it. Nurses. Doctors. Random people passing by in the hallway. Everyone seemed to be discussing the kidnapping, the car wreck that had killed the kidnapper, the state trooper who'd happened upon Portia and Katie as they made their escape. God's handiwork. That's what people were saying and Portia agreed. She'd been stiff with cold when the police cruiser sped by, so cold she could barely lift an arm to wave for help. That he'd spotted them and returned was a gift from God, one she'd always be grateful for.

"This will sting just a bit." The hypodermic needle the physician's assistant held looked like it would sting more than a little.

"Are stitches really necessary?" Portia glanced at the deep cut on the palm of her hand and decided she'd be better off not looking again.

"After the experience you've been through, I can't believe you're worried about a needle. It's hard to believe that a man could hold a grudge for so long, isn't it? That he'd come back and kill someone out of revenge?"

Portia winced as the needle found its mark. "What do you mean?"

"You haven't heard yet? The guy who grabbed you was an ex-con. The police searched his apartment and found antidepressants and alcohol. The same combo that killed Garrett McGraw."

"He knew Garrett McGraw?" Portia's relief at knowing her father wasn't a murderer almost outweighed the pain of the second needle.

"Knew him? McGraw was one of the guys responsible for him being in jail. He and Mick Campbell worked together in Portland. Guess this guy, Zimmerman, was determined to get back at both the cops who nabbed him."

"Mick and Garrett worked together?"

"Yeah, McGraw was a police officer before he moved back here. He didn't talk about it much, just said he preferred small-town life to city living. He and Campbell were partners before he came back home."

"Partners?" So that was the truth Mick was hiding. For some reason, he hadn't wanted Portia to know how deep the connection was between himself and Garrett. It shouldn't have hurt, but it did. She'd shared so much of herself, let him see her deepest fears and closest-held dreams.

And he couldn't even tell her the truth about something as simple as this.

Portia thought back over their conversations, remembered the moments of hesitation when she'd asked about Garrett. He'd had opportunities, plenty of them, to tell her the truth, but he hadn't. Why not?

And did the answer even matter?

"You okay? You're looking a little green around the gills. You're not the kind to faint at the sight of blood, are you?"

"No. I'm fine. It's just been a long day." Her throat was raw and sore, her heart heavy.

"I bet. Getting attacked, saving Katie Campbell." The PA shook her head. "That little girl is in great shape, thanks to you. I know her father is ecstatic to have her back unharmed."

"I'm sure."

"We're almost done here. One more stitch and I'll bandage the wound. Your aunt and sister are out in the waiting area. Want me to send them in when I'm finished?"

"Yes. Thanks."

But Portia didn't bother waiting. As soon as the PA left the room, she stood, pulled on the jacket she'd been given by the officer who'd brought her to the hospital and walked out into the corridor.

Aunt Winnie and Miranda were both there. They looked up, saw Portia and rushed to drag her into their arms. It felt good to be there, good to know her family was safe, that Garrett's murderer had been found, that her father was in the clear and she knew she should be happy. Instead, she felt empty and much older than her twenty-six years.

"Are you okay?" Miranda whispered in her ear, never easing the bear hug she was holding Portia in. "We've been worried sick."

"I'm okay."

"Then let's get you home."

Portia nodded and allowed herself to be ushered away. She didn't—wouldn't—look for Mick.

TWENTY-FIVE

"So, do you think you're going to stop moping anytime soon? Because, if this were a play, I'd be getting a little bored about now." Rissa slapped a paper bag on the break table in the arts and crafts store and shot Portia a concerned look.

"I'm not moping."

"No? Then what do you call it?"

"I'm…" Portia smiled, hoping she wouldn't look as gloomy as she felt. "Moping. But I'll get over it." Eventually.

"Get over *him,* you mean. I brought you ham on rye." She gestured to the bag. "You'd better eat fast. Your next class starts in ten minutes."

"I asked Cara to take it."

"Again?" Rissa sat across from Portia. The break room at the art studio was just big enough for a table and chairs; it wasn't fancy, but Portia had always liked the cozy comfort of it. Now, it just felt crowded and claustrophobic.

"My hand is still bothering me."

"You got the stitches out three days ago."

"And it's bothering me." That much was true. The cut

on her palm had been deep and difficult to heal, though she had to admit the pain wasn't enough to keep her from demonstrating jewelry-making techniques. She just couldn't find the energy to face her ten students.

Rissa took a bite out of her sandwich. "I've seen you work with blisters on both hands, so I'm not buying that story. Admit it, Portia, you don't want to be back in New York. You'd rather be in Stoneley."

"I'd rather have answers to the questions we've all been asking. Does Father know more about Mother than he's saying? Did he know she was alive all those years? If Mother is alive, where is she now? Why hasn't she ever tried to see us? No matter how hard I try not to think about those things, I can't help wondering and I can't help needing to know the answers."

"So go find them."

"It's not as easy as that."

"Why not? Because you made a mistake and you're afraid you've ruined everything?" Rissa's face softened. "So what if you ran away without saying goodbye to Mick and his daughter? That's not a good reason to stay away."

"That makes me feel so much better, Sis."

"Hey, I'm only telling you what we both know. You want to go back, but you're afraid you blew it with Mick."

In a way it was true. Portia might be upset that Mick hadn't told her the truth about Garrett McGraw, but she'd still thought about going home to Stoneley a thousand times since she'd returned to New York two weeks before. She missed Mick, but that wasn't something she planned to share with Rissa. Doing so would make her look even more pitiful than she already did. "I'm not afraid I blew it. I'm just not sure I want to go back to Stoneley. There are so many other places in the world.

Once the sale of the store is finalized, I'll find one of them and make a new start."

Rissa finished her sandwich and stood, shooting Portia a look filled with both amusement and frustration. "I love you to pieces, but you're too smart to be acting so dumb about this. Stoneley is your place. It always has been. Go find it. Go find *Mick*."

"Go find Mick? After he lied to me?" She wanted to feel anger, but it wasn't there. Everything she'd learned about Mick, everything she'd seen of him, told her he'd had a reason for what he'd done and everything inside of her told her she should have stayed around to find out what that reason was.

"He didn't tell you everything. That's not the same as lying. He's a cop. There were probably things he couldn't tell you even if he'd wanted to."

"I know," Portia sighed, rubbed at the tension in her neck. "The fact is, I've thought about calling him a million times. I don't know what to say. *Why'd you lie? I'm sorry I didn't say goodbye?*"

"Maybe both those things. Maybe more." Rissa stood and stretched. "Listen, we have a guest signed up for your jewelry class. He seemed like an interesting guy. I think you'd like to meet him. Wait here. I'll send him back."

"I'm not up to—" But her sister was already gone, striding down the corridor and out the door that led to the shop and classroom. Portia leaned a shoulder against the wall and waited, hoping the new student would be a no-show and she could go home. The door swung open and someone stepped into the hallway—tall with broad shoulders and a long-legged stride. Mick.

Portia's heart jumped and she put her hands behind her back to keep from reaching for him. He stepped close, his jaw tight, his eyes flashing with irritation and something that looked like worry.

Portia wanted to smooth the lines from his brow, smooth the frown from his lips. "Mick, what are you doing here?"

"I needed to talk to you about a couple things."

"You could have called." But she was so glad he hadn't.

"I could have, but I thought it would be better to bring you this news in person."

"News?"

"Two things. The first is that we traced the phone call Zimmerman made when he was outside the cabin, but the number he called was a cell phone that was also in his name."

"So you have no way to trace the person he called."

"Unfortunately, no. For now, we're working under the assumption that he had an accomplice and we're doing everything we can to find out who that person was."

"It can't happen too quickly."

"Agreed. The only good news is that the threats against my family have stopped and things in Stoneley seem to be back to normal."

"That is good news." But from the look on Mick's face, the rest of what he had to tell her wasn't so good. "What else?"

"I've got some news about your mother."

Her mother? It was the last thing Portia expected to hear. Her heart raced with dread, anticipation. "Tell me."

"A few years ago your grandfather named your father CEO of Blanchard Fabrics."

"That's right. Grandfather had been diagnosed with Alzheimer's. He felt that letting Father take over would be for the best."

"Your father listed you and your sisters as heirs to his majority stocks in the company."

"That's not a surprise."

"No, but my partner Drew found something else that was. A signed document relinquishing Trudy Blanchard's parental rights, dated a year after her supposed death."

"Are you sure?" Portia's heart thudded, her mind numb with the realization that what she'd suspected about her father was true. He'd been lying for years, keeping Portia and her sisters from their mother.

"I wouldn't be here if I weren't."

"Thank you for telling me." She brushed past, not wanting him to see the tears in her eyes. "I've got to go tell Rissa."

Before she could take a step, his hand closed over hers and he pulled her back around to face him. "You're running away again."

"How could I be? I didn't run away the first time."

"No? Then why did you leave without saying goodbye?"

"I needed time to think."

"About?"

"About—about you never mentioning that you and Garrett were partners." There. It was out. And Mick didn't look at all surprised to hear it.

"And are you done thinking?" He ran a hand down his jaw, his eyes dark and simmering with banked emotion.

"Does it matter? You came to tell me about my mother. I appreciate it. Isn't that enough?"

"If it were, I would have called you on the phone and saved myself the flight here."

"Mick—"

"Don't tell me that you don't feel what I do. That there isn't something more between us than friendship, or me doing my job or you looking for your mother." He tugged her closer, stared down into her eyes and Portia felt the world shrink to that one moment. That one man.

"I wasn't going to."

"Yes, you were. Because that would be easier than admitting that I hurt you. That you trusted me and I broke that trust."

"Trust? I don't even know what that means anymore."

"Don't you? Then I'll tell you. It means being able to count on someone else. It means knowing that what a person says is what he's going to do. It means knowing that when I tell you something, it's the truth." He smoothed his hands down her shoulders, linked fingers with hers. "And you *can* trust me, Portia."

"How can I, when you didn't trust me enough to tell me everything about Garrett McGraw?"

"That wasn't about not trusting you. It was about a promise I made. Eight years ago Garrett McGraw was kicked off the Portland police department for police brutality. It was my testimony to Internal Affairs that caused that to happen and I've always felt guilty about it. When I returned to Stoneley, McGraw asked me not to tell anyone. He'd built a life for himself, had a wife and kids. Everyone in town believed he'd quit the force because he missed small-town life. He wanted to keep it that way. For the sake of his family and because I felt I owed him something, I promised to keep quiet. If you'd given me a chance, I would have told you. I'd planned to tell you the day you and Katie were kidnapped. Then things went crazy and it was too late."

Portia gazed into Mick's eyes, heard the ring of truth

in his voice and wondered how she ever could have doubted him. "I think I knew that."

"Then why'd you run?"

"You seemed too good to be true. I guess I figured you were."

"If you'd stuck around, you would have realized I don't actually seem all that good." He smiled and all Portia's anxiety melted away.

"If I'd stayed, I wouldn't have had time to figure out what I really want from life."

"You've had two weeks. Was that enough time to figure it out?" His fingers brushed the curls that lay against her cheek.

"Yes. I think it was."

"I don't suppose you'd like to share?" He cupped her face in his hands, his eyes the clear, crisp blue of spring, with just as much promise.

"Sure. I don't want anything big. A new store in a small town, a house with a yard and a fence. Maybe even a dog."

"Sounds nice."

"There's more."

"Yeah?"

"Yeah. A man who accepts me just the way I am, who knows me well and loves me anyway. A precious little girl with an eye for jewelry. A beautiful horizon with all the colors of the rainbow in it."

"Sounds like a tall order."

"Yeah? Well, you're a pretty tall guy."

"I guess I am." He smiled and tugged her into his arms. "But you know, I have a few things I want, too."

"Do you?"

"Yep. A house. A fence. Maybe even a dog."

"I like the sound of that."

"And a woman who is sure to drive me absolutely crazy with her stubborn determination, but who will always have my back. A woman just like you." Mick captured her lips with his, the warmth of his embrace filling Portia with joy. Whatever the future brought, whatever the truth about her father and her mother, Portia knew Mick would be at her side, steady and sure, a wonderful gift from God who held every moment in the palm of His hand.

* * * * *

Dear Reader,

Families create the very fabric of who we are. Whether we are living up to the example our family has set, or striving to create something better than what we had growing up, we can't deny that we've been molded and changed by our families.

One of six sisters, Portia Blanchard loves her unconventional family. When a P.I. her sister hired is murdered, she's determined to prove that her family is innocent of the crime. To do that, she must learn to trust police detective Mick Campbell, a man who is just as determined to prove the Blanchards guilty.

I hope you enjoy their adventure! And I hope that as you read you'll think about your faith and the path you're traveling. May it lead wherever God desires you to be, and may it be filled with the joy and laughter of family.

I love to hear from readers. You can reach me at shirlee@shirleemccoy.com.

All His best,

Shirlee McCoy

QUESTIONS FOR DISCUSSION

1. In the first chapter of *Little Girl Lost,* we meet the six Blanchard sisters and gain insight into the role each plays in the family. Based on the first scene, what role does Portia have in her family?

2. How does Portia's role change as the story progresses?

3. During the course of the book it becomes obvious that some of Portia's sisters aren't quite as enthusiastic about the yearly reunion as she is. Why do you think Portia worries about her sisters' lack of enthusiasm and commitment? What does she think this says about her family?

4. What deep-rooted fears cause Portia to cling so tenaciously to the Winter Festival tradition?

5. As her faith grows, Portia is able to release some of these fears. How does that have an impact on her relationship with family members?

6. As Christians, we believe that having a relationship with Christ leads to completion, rightness in life and confidence in our place in the world. However, despite our faith, we often struggle to find those things. Portia struggles with the same. As a child, "she'd dreamed of leaving the Manor, of making a name for herself." As an adult she realizes that those things have done nothing to fulfill her. What is it Portia is really seeking? How does she finally find it?

7. As a widower and father, Mick's first priority is to his daughter. How does he balance that with his growing feelings for Portia?

8. Mick's marriage wasn't what he'd hoped for. What was it about his marriage that threatened to destroy it? How does that affect Mick's perception of and feelings for Portia?

9. The underlying tension in this book revolves around the mystery concerning Portia's mother. How does Ronald Blanchard's deception regarding the matter have an impact on Portia's relationship with Mick?

10. Portia feels that she's been betrayed and lied to by both her father and grandfather. Her ex-boyfriend did the same. Still, she is able to put those betrayals aside and embrace a relationship with Mick. How? What is it that helps her move beyond hurt and pain and into the future God has planned for her?

Coming to work for Blanchard Fabrics was supposed to bring Juliet Blanchard closer to her distant father. But it brought her close to Brandon De Witte, a handsome man with many secrets. Would Brandon's search for family vengeance lead to the destruction of Blanchard Fabrics? Find out in Terri Reed's BELOVED ENEMY....

And now, turn the page for a sneak preview of BELOVED ENEMY, the third installment of The Secrets of Stoneley

On sale in March 2007 from Steeple Hill Books

Not sure what she was looking for or where she'd find it, Juliet began with the books on the shelves in the attic. Methodically, she pulled each one out, thumbed through the pages and shook them to see if anything lay hidden between the pages. Near the bottom shelf, she found a cardboard box behind a layer of books—a box she'd never seen before.

Moving the books aside, she pulled the box off the shelf. It was a bit heavy as if more were inside. Gently setting it on the floor so as not to make a noise that would alert anyone on the floor below of her presence, Juliet sat down beside it. The top was taped shut. Using her fingernail, she poked and peeled at the aged, yellow tape. When she had broken through the seal on the four sides, she lifted the lid.

Just as she suspected, the box was full of books. Textbooks. But whose?

She examined each of them. Under one textbook was a class schedule with the name Trudy Blanchard on it. Ah. These had been her mother's books from when she'd gone back to college to become a teacher, right before she'd gotten pregnant with Juliet. Had Trudy not finished college because she was pregnant? Had the thwarted dream of being a teacher contributed to her mother's postpartum depression?

Her mother had once touched these books. Juliet's heart squeezed with sorrow for having never known the woman who'd given her life.

That kicked-in-the-gut feeling Juliet always experienced when she thought about her mother's reasons for abandoning her family—and her subsequent "death"—hit Juliet hard now. One more heartbreak her birth was responsible for.

She wiped at the tear sliding down her cheek. Self-pity wasn't going to help. Bianca was convinced Trudy was alive. Until they all knew for sure one way or the other, Juliet had to stay focused on helping to bring closure for the sisters she loved.

And for herself.

The last book in the box was her mother's college yearbook. Juliet hugged it to her chest for a moment before opening the cover and searching through the pages for her mother's picture. Finding it, she traced a fingertip over the small square photo. Her pretty green eyes sparkled; her blond hair was cut in a trendy bob. The camera captured her playful smile. A smile Juliet never had the privilege of knowing.

She shut the book and laid it aside so she could refill the box with the textbooks. She'd take the yearbook to her room to show the others in the morning. She was sure they'd want to see another aspect of their mother. After arranging the box just as she'd found it, she picked up the yearbook. Something from between the pages fluttered to the floor.

Blinking, Juliet stared at the photo lying face up on the ground. Squatting and setting the yearbook down, she gaped at the dog-eared picture of her mother, arm-in-arm with a slightly older man. Her mother's face so happy and carefree, her slim frame clad in a full skirt and pink sweater. The man wore brown slacks and an argyle sweater-vest over a button-down shirt. The couple stood on the steps of the local college's campus entrance, and from the way they gazed into each other's eyes, it was clear they had feelings for one another.

Juliet sat down. Her heart hammered in her chest. This had to be from the first time Trudy had attended college. Did her sisters know their mother had had a boyfriend before she'd married their father?

Juliet flipped the picture over with the tip of a fingernail. Her mouth went dry and she began to shake. Written in a neat script that was not her mother's were the words, "Yours always and forever, Arthur."

But it was the date tidily penned in the corner that sucked the breath from her lungs. A day approximately a year prior to Juliet's birth.

The photo was not from Trudy's first years of college, but from the second time she'd enrolled, which seemed to suggest that her mother had been involved with another man while married to Ronald Blanchard.

Grabbing the photo with shaky hands, Juliet turned it over again to stare at the man in the photo. She blinked several times to clear her mind, because what she was seeing couldn't be true. She slowly rose and moved to stand in front of the floor-length mirror. Her reflection was muted from the aging glass, but what she saw didn't deny what her head didn't want to accept.

She bore an uncanny resemblance to the man in the photo. It was there in the line of his nose and the shape of his jaw, much like her own.

Her mind jumped and skidded to a conclusion that weakened her knees.

Could this mystery man be her biological father?

She whirled away from the mirror and rushed back to the yearbook. Frantically, she searched every page for more pictures of the man named Arthur, but there were none.

Mind reeling and heart racing, she sank to the floor. Was the reason she'd always felt like an outsider because she was not Ronald Blanchard's daughter? Was that why Ronald stayed so emotionally detached from his youngest child?

The conclusion made sense.

A silent wail ran through her body, making her shudder as the dream of having Ronald's love cracked.

But how would she tell her sisters she might not be one of them?

Love Inspired®
SUSPENSE
RIVETING INSPIRATIONAL ROMANCE

Don't miss the intrigue and the romance
in this six-book family saga.

THE SECRETS
OF STONELEY

**Six sisters face murder, mayhem
and mystery while unraveling the past.**

FATAL IMAGE
Lenora Worth
January 2007

**THE SOUND
OF SECRETS**
Irene Brand
April 2007

LITTLE GIRL LOST
Shirlee McCoy
February 2007

DEADLY PAYOFF
Valerie Hansen
May 2007

BELOVED ENEMY
Terri Reed
March 2007

**WHERE THE
TRUTH LIES**
Lynn Bulock
June 2007

Steeple
Hill®

Available wherever you buy books.

www.SteepleHill.com

LISSOSLIST

REQUEST YOUR FREE BOOKS!

2 FREE INSPIRATIONAL NOVELS
PLUS 2
FREE
MYSTERY GIFTS

Love Inspired

YES! Please send me 2 FREE Love Inspired® novels and my 2 FREE mystery gifts. After receiving them, if I don't wish to receive any more books, I can return the shipping statement marked "cancel." If I don't cancel, I will receive 4 brand-new novels every month and be billed just $3.99 per book in the U.S., or $4.74 per book in Canada, plus 25¢ shipping and handling per book and applicable taxes, if any*. That's a savings of 20% off the cover price! I understand that accepting the 2 free books and gifts places me under no obligation to buy anything. I can always return a shipment and cancel at any time. Even if I never buy another book from Steeple Hill, the two free books and gifts are mine to keep forever.

113 IDN EF26 313 IDN EF27

Name	(PLEASE PRINT)
Address	Apt. #
City	State/Prov.	Zip/Postal Code

Signature (if under 18, a parent or guardian must sign)

Order online at www.LoveInspiredBooks.com

Or mail to Steeple Hill Reader Service™:

IN U.S.A.: P.O. Box 1867, Buffalo, NY 14240-1867
IN CANADA: P.O. Box 609, Fort Erie, Ontario L2A 5X3

Not valid to current Love Inspired subscribers.

Want to try two free books from another series?
Call 1-800-873-8635 or visit www.morefreebooks.com

* Terms and prices subject to change without notice. NY residents add applicable sales tax. Canadian residents will be charged applicable provincial taxes and GST. This offer is limited to one order per household. All orders subject to approval. Credit or debit balances in a customer's account(s) may be offset by any other outstanding balance owed by or to the customer. Please allow 4 to 6 weeks for delivery.

Your Privacy: Steeple Hill is committed to protecting your privacy. Our Privacy Policy is available online at www.eHarlequin.com or upon request from the Reader Service. From time to time we make our lists of customers available to reputable firms who may have a product or service of interest to you. If you would prefer we not share your name and address, please check here. ☐

LIREG07

Love Inspired
SUSPENSE

TITLES AVAILABLE NEXT MONTH

Don't miss these four stories in March

SO DARK THE NIGHT by Margaret Daley

On a tragic night, photographer Emma St. James
lost her vision and her memory of her brother's murder.
She was alone on the run from the killers, until Reverend
Colin Fitzpatrick reached out with a touch she couldn't
see....

BELOVED ENEMY by Terri Reed
The Secrets of Stoneley

Juliet Blanchard stumbled upon a picture that cast doubt on
her parentage. With the world crumbling around her, could
she trust handsome newcomer Brandon DeWitte to help her
find the truth without breaking her heart?

SHADOWS OF TRUTH by Sharon Mignerey

Only one thing could bring DEA agent Micah McLeod back to
Carbondale, Colorado: Rachel Neesham was in danger. He'd
vowed to keep her and her two children safe at any cost.
Would Rachel let him? Her life depended on it.

PURSUIT OF JUSTICE by Pamela Tracy

While helping the police bust a drug ring, Rosa Cagnalia
found herself framed for murder. Officer Samuel Packard
suspected that Rosa might be innocent. Now if only he could
get his beautiful suspect to cooperate...